SUCCUMBING TO SCARS AND SORROW

SUCCUMBING TO SCARS AND SORROW

Book One of the Sorrow Series

Mary E. Palmerin

Archway Publishing books may be ordered through booksellers or by contacting:

Archway Publishing
1663 Liberty Drive
Bloomington, IN 47403
www.archwaypublishing.com
1-(888)-242-5904

ISBN: 978-1-4808-0198-1 (sc)
ISBN: 978-1-4808-0200-1 (hc)
ISBN: 978-1-4808-0199-8 (e)

Library of Congress Control Number: 2013914850

Printed in the United States of America

Archway Publishing rev. date: 08/15/13

To my mother, Lee Ann Kipta, and my Aunt, Teri Rose. Without both of you, I wouldn't have been able to write Lyla's story. Also, to my grandparents, Patricia and Donald "Bud" Rose. I know you guys are proud of me for following my dreams and are smiling down from heaven. All of you have always encouraged me to follow my dreams and my heart. This book is for all of you. I love you!

Most of all, I thank God. Without Him, I would not be able to live my dream and trust my heart!

Acknowledgments

To my husband, Domingo, for encouraging me through the process of writing this book. I have been in love with you since I was eighteen.

To my two amazing kids, Cruz and Lincoln. I love you both more than life, and I hope one day to support you in any endeavor that you choose. If I could give you any advice, it would be to follow your heart and chase your dreams. Life is too short to live it otherwise.

Many thanks to the people that have encouraged me through the process of writing this book, especially my cousins, Stephanie Wagner and Ashley Rudisill. Without your support, endless random phone calls, and good advice, I would not have been able to do this.

To my longtime friend and amazing tattoo artist, Khristian Seaton, for listening to my life and stories and pushing me to follow my dreams. You rock! You have created an amazing cover for my book! I am so glad to be able to have you as a friend and I am excited to be a part of your career. It will take you far.

To my dear friend and fellow author of *Whatever it Takes*, L. Maretta, I thank you from the bottom of my heart for being a genuine friend to me! You have given me amazing advice, and I am eternally grateful.

Thanks to Luke Rudisill for giving me legal advice. You are great!

To my brother, John Kipta, and sister, Catherine Neff, for always letting me be "me" ... the baby of the family! We love hard, fight hard, and make up hard. I love you both more than words!

To the rest of my family ... I love you all. Thank you from the bottom of my heart for the support, honesty, and love you have given me throughout the years.

I am so grateful to be able to start telling Lyla and Everett's story. I hope you all continue to follow up with their life in Book Two of the Sorrow Series, *Shadows of Scars and Sorrow*.

Chapter 1

THE DAY BEGAN as most did. I awoke feeling slightly sour, my mood the result of last night's binge. I was imprisoned by the ferocious downward spiral that had consumed my life and altered it forever. I was convinced that it wasn't worth caring about—my life, that is. I was used to disappointing myself and all the people I loved so much. It hurt the greatest to see the people who meant a lot to me living in constant turmoil.

I was like a tigress whose stripes would remain the same for eternity. I was sure that my life would be unsatisfactory and I would die alone with a closet full of skeletons and many regrets. Since I lost my innocence, things went downhill. I was absolutely certain that I was in the murkiest of disconsolate places and that there would never be any faith in my future.

I staggered out of bed feeling a cold chill shoot through the pads of my feet into my legs like a blast of lightning. The emotional pain was manifesting into physical pain, something I grew accustomed to over the past several years, whether it was self-induced or not.

Moments later, I found myself in the bathroom and splashed cool water on my face, eager to feel revitalized. Too bad that also proved to be ineffective. The dark, sad circles remained beneath my bright brown eyes. That low-spirited cloud of gray had lurked over my body and somehow had seared the effects into my olive complexion.

I left the bathroom and wrapped my favorite pink, knee-length, fuzzy robe over my scarred and broken body. I then headed down my narrow hallway and into my tiny kitchen to start my Keurig coffee maker and light my morning cigarette.

I proceeded to check my phone to see if I had sent any text messages or made any calls that I would have to be repentant for. Thankfully I hadn't. I poured my hazelnut-flavored coffee into my beloved pink china coffee cup with matching saucer that my grandmother had given me months before she died. For a few seconds, a crooked smile appeared at the edges of my mouth with the sweet memories of my aging grandmother and her tiny, wrinkled, loving hands.

"*Ti amo di piu,*" she would say to me.

I would then reply, "No, Nonie, I love you more!"

Memories of my grandmother always brought me back to my happy place.

I added cream and sugar to my coffee, stirring carefully so I would not spill the hot contents on the perfectly hand-painted pink heirloom saucer. I lit another Parliament and took a long drag, contemplating the upcoming day. *No failure!* I yelled in my head. *You can do this. Prove yourself and everyone wrong,* I chanted to myself again.

I felt as if I had no choice but to feel determination, to set off my attitude and fill it positively, unlike my usual pessimistic one; trusting the newness of my future would change the aura that had shadowed me for what seemed like eons. This would be my last chance for something genuinely good and normal.

My mind was racing with thoughts of how my first day would go. I had just graduated from Loyola University with a degree in public relations and marketing. I had landed an internship at a prestigious public relations and marketing firm. It was going to be my last chance to try to believe in myself. I was going to try my best to make something good out of years of bad.

It was amazing that I had managed to stay in school and make halfway decent grades. That was important to my parents, and that must have been the only thing I had managed to do right in some time. I loved portraying a smart and organized woman who was good with other people. Surprisingly, I was honest at reading others and made respectable business decisions.

Even if I was alone for the rest of my life (because of my past, I was certain this would be true), I wanted something to be proud of. Even if it wasn't me, I figured I would try to center it around my career. I would try my damnedest to be the best at what I learned in school. Put my skills to use and move up into the advertising world. Fill my hours with work so I wouldn't have to think of all the unhappiness that had taken such a large chunk out of my life.

I was fucked up, and no one could fix me. I could not even repair myself, though I'm not sure how much I tried. Deep down I was ready for something spectacular to happen. But I was used to only seeing that in movies and reading it in romance novels and was sure there was never going to be a happily ever after for me.

I could settle for a seventy-hour work week with little sleep and spending Saturday nights with a nice bottle of shiraz and Lifetime movies in my favorite sweat pants and tank top. "Accept it, Lyla," I said to myself once more.

I continuously had dreams of getting out of the shitty little Midwestern town that I grew up in. Thinking of Rigdon, Kansas, made my stomach churn with the horrid memories that I left behind and hadn't revisited in four years. It was the type of town where everyone knew everything about all and sundry. It was all about who's who and where the money was and who had the greatest of it.

I was lucky that my mother married into it. He was a good man, and I considered him my father. I had given him more grief than he deserved. He was decent to me, and I hadn't seen it until it was close to being too late.

My mother was an outstanding woman. She was the one I could always count on. No matter what, I knew she loved me, but I always ended up not satisfying her. I was trusting that my internship would turn things around, not only for me, but for all those I had let down. I wanted to prove everyone wrong.

Enough thinking of the past, I thought. It was time to get ready for the newest adventure of my wayward life. I walked into my tiny bathroom and turned on the shower, full hotness to wash away what I had been trying to for years. I opened the shower curtain and lodged myself into the tub, letting the hot water tread down all my curves, trying not to think of anything.

As much as I tried, I always failed, and I felt the tears pool in my eyes. I stopped myself this morning. I didn't want my eyes to be swollen from the tears, so I took a few seconds to compose myself and finished up cleaning my physically and emotionally scarred body.

I stepped out of the shower, wiped the fog off the mirror, and glowered at my naked body, hating every inch of myself. I touched the scars that covered most of the surface of my stomach and winced at the recollections.

People had told me I was pretty, but I never saw it. My size-12 hips, full breasts, and backside always had me self-conscious since the Marilyn Monroe body was no longer in and anorexic was. I was curvy and voluptuous. Maybe that was because most of my supposed friends back at home were blonde and size 0. That just wasn't me. Of course I strived to be such and always came back dissatisfied.

I rubbed lotion on my olive-toned skin, pleased with all my tattoos. My favorite one was between my shoulder blades that read *Only God Can Judge Me* in Hebrew. I did love my skin and all my body art. I had a large pink lotus flower covering the right side of my rib cage and *The Virgin Mary* along the latter half of my back. I got my skin tone from my mother's family; they were Sicilian.

I dressed in my black pencil skirt and white blouse and put on my red pumps that matched my fire-red lipstick. I applied jet-black eyeliner and black mascara. I decided to pull my long, black hair into a sleek ponytail and be on my way to the newest venture of my life.

I wasn't all that frightened about starting my internship. I was optimistic that it would put some sort of light back into my life. I grabbed my keys and stepped out of my apartment. I filled my lungs with the crisp autumn air.

I got in my old 1997 Toyota Corolla and started the engine. I turned on my iPod, deciding to listen to one of my favorite artists, Kate Nash. My mind began to wander as I thought about what I truly wanted in life.

I hadn't made it to Manhattan yet. That was where my dreams always took me. I came to the conclusion that I should take baby steps. After all, I was interning at the largest public relations and marketing firm in Chicago. That wasn't too shabby. I never gave myself credit; I did, if nothing else, migrate from a tiny southeastern Kansas town to Chicago. That had to mean something.

I felt the buzzing sound in my purse as I was trying to park my car in a massive parking garage. The vibrating was then followed by Adele's *Chasing Pavements*. I had that as my ringtone, and it seemed fit to my life.

I answered with an exasperated, "Hello?"

"Hey, my sweet princess! Just wanted to wish you good luck today. I know you'll do great!" said my mom in an ever so sweet tone.

"Thanks, Mom. I'm running a little behind, trying to find a parking spot. Can I give you a call when I get settled?"

"Sure, honey, just when you get time. Kisses and hugs. I miss you. I love you, my darling daughter."

She always had a way of making me feel restored. Her voice alone could bring a smile to my face. I stuffed my phone back into my purse as I found a spot and claimed it. I had grit running through my veins, willpower to change my shitty outlook on life.

The skyscraper was huge, and if you looked all the way up to the top, you could feel your neck strain. I was a few minutes early, which was better than being late. I needed to be at the twenty-eighth floor in fifteen minutes.

I straightened my skirt, dabbed some more red lipstick on my lips, and checked myself in the side mirror of my car. I then started walking into the place that could potentially change me and make my life worth something. I was ready for something, anything good to change me. I wanted to change me.

Chapter 2

I ENTERED THE enormous building, completely awed by what was going on around me. Attractive businessmen were everywhere, talking into their earpieces. None of them looked happy; they appeared hurried. Beautiful women in Prada suits were carrying on with the same motions. I headed toward the main elevator and pushed the up button, taking one last deep breath.

After what seemed like forever, I made it to the twenty-eighth floor. I greeted the receptionist with a fake smile.

"Hello. You must be Lyla Harper. I'm Estelle, and Mr. Michael Thomas will be with you shortly," she said curtly.

"Yes, thank you," I replied with the forged smile still on my face.

For a brief moment, I was puzzled as to how she knew who I was. I dismissed the idea and tried focusing on the energetic office full of tiny cubicles and bustling employees.

She took me through the office, weaving in and out of workspaces. All employees were at their desks doing their jobs diligently. It would be a wonder if I remembered where to go tomorrow. I was trying to pay attention, trying my best to make things work out, hoping with all my being that this could be the turning point of my life.

I settled into a tiny compartment near a large office that consisted of all windows. Considering where the rest of the cubicles were located, I had front-row seats. I had a nice view and was sure that the individual that occupied the enormous office had to be someone very important. That person had to be the infamous Mr. Michael Thomas.

I took some time to look into his office from my work area. There was a large mahogany desk that occupied a colossal space in front of the windows that overlooked downtown Chicago. It was accompanied by a black leather high-back swivel chair.

A great black leather sofa sat at the opposite end of the office with a huge flat-screen plasma television mounted on the wall with CNN on. There was a bar in the corner, something I thought ad execs had only had back in the fifties. Apparently it was still appropriate to drink on the job when you were the boss.

I was assigned to be an assistant to Mr. Michael Thomas, a public relations and marketing mogul known to be a millionaire and a jerk. I could get past that. I was used to dealing with difficult people—the ostensible acquaintances and friends I had back in Rigdon. They were bitches and assholes, no one I could trust, but I always smiled and tried to fit in.

A tall, muscular man with salt and pepper hair and defined cheekbones sauntered over to me. "Coffee, two creams one sugar—now. Then into my office," he snapped.

Wow, he was a dick. I stood quickly, finding the break room as fast as I could. I poured his coffee like I was told and found my way back into his office.

"You must be Lyla Harper. I'm Mr. Thomas. That is what you will call me. I will go over my expectations from you. As long as you do what you are told, things should work out around here," he said.

"Nice to meet you, Mr. Thomas," I said politely with a smile, showing off my fire-red lipstick and pearly white teeth.

"I expect coffee on my desk every morning the way I like it. I told you how I want it, and I shouldn't have to tell you again. You will fetch me lunch every day. Here is a list of restaurants and items I want from each one. You will have a copy of my schedule and know the days I have lunches planned. Those days, I won't need you to get me anything. You are to dress in skirts and tight blouses as you have today. You are to answer my phone like it is the happiest day in your life. Do we have an understanding?"

I was absolutely shocked but replied, "Yes, sir."

"I thought I told you to refer to me as Mr. Thomas," he said, sounding annoyed.

"Of course, Mr. Thomas" I said, still stunned at his expectations.

Skirts and tight blouses? You've got to be kidding me. Is he really a pervert? Was I really getting myself into a similar situation again? His perverted, cocky demeanor would get to me; that was undisputable. I had to overcome it. After all, I was ready to adjust my life, to pick up the pieces and show everyone I could transform into the person they desired.

I did as I was told and answered the phone favorably each time it rang. I organized his schedule and did all the duties that were part of my job. I was willing to learn from this internship. A girl had to start somewhere.

It was nearing five o'clock, and I was ready for my first day to be over. It went as smoothly as any first day had. I was structured, so that worked in my benefit. Mr. I'm an Asshole Pervert made his way to my desk.

"You survived your first day. I suppose you will do. Continue doing as you are told, and everything should work out. My office— now," he said in a voice that shook me to my core.

I got up as I was told and entered his throne room. That was how it appeared because most of the day he sat there drinking his amber-colored liquor while watching CNN and CSPAN.

"Sit," he said. I sat in one of the leather chairs parallel to his desk.

He stared at me for a moment.

"Do you have a boyfriend?" he asked in a friendly tone.

"No, Mr. Thomas," I answered, trying to withhold the utter disbelief in my voice. I felt my heart skip a beat. I mentally composed myself, unwilling to allow this asshole boss of mine to affect me.

"Good, then you are definitely a keeper. You may go now. Remember what I said about your wardrobe. I have expectations, and I expect you to meet every single one of them. You are curvier than I imagined but striking indeed. I cannot have you looking shabby. Dress to impress, Miss Harper."

"Yes, sir—I mean Mr. Thomas," I replied, still trying to process his requests. I'd be damned to continue to attract such douche bag-perverts. What. The. Fuck.

"Good. Now go."

I couldn't believe what had transpired. I guessed I would have to deal with it. It was the way for me to pick up the shards that had taken all my life to break. It was not all my fault. Years of counseling had convinced me of that, but a lot was my doing (at least that's what I thought). I had to fix what I had damaged. I had to patch up the bridges I had burned. I was going to do it no matter what it took. I made my way out of the skyscraper that looked as if it stretched a million miles into the sky.

I got into my car, and my annoying phone started buzzing, playing the ringtone *Chasing Pavements*.

"Hello?" I said, my pissed-off, pessimistic view still shadowing me.

"Hey, girl, how was your first day? Want to meet for a drink?" It was Anya Ross, a friend I met at school.

Of course she was gorgeous, always showing off her platinum blonde hair, blue eyes, perky tits, and perfect figure. She never made me feel self-conscious because she wasn't that type of person; trust me I could decipher one because I had come into contact with plenty in my twenty-three years of existence.

Anya was the one person that I could halfway trust in Chicago. She was a true friend. I didn't feel like being social but agreed to meet her, hoping to put the first day behind me. I hoped that distracting myself in a social atmosphere would put the anxiety and dooming thoughts aside, at least for a little while.

Thinking of my boss made the thoughts of the *problem* I left behind in Rigdon, Kansas, resurface. I had to dismiss them before they affected me in a negative way. It had been years since I regressed into my old ways. Hopefully I would be strong enough not to go back to my old way of dealing with things. I could pray.

Anya and I had met in one of our prerequisite classes freshman year. She was majoring in political science and was applying to every prestigious law school you could imagine. She was not only pretty but amazingly smart too. She had it all. I envied her for that but never let it show. She was a good listener and a good friend.

I met her at a low-key piano bar. It had a pleasant atmosphere, and the music was low enough that you could still hold a decent conversation and hear the person you were speaking with.

"Hey!" Anya said with a big, white, perfect-teeth smile. I waved nonchalantly, trying to put on a happy front and dismiss the negative cloud of gray that had followed me for as long as I could remember.

We sat in the corner of the bar on a bistro-like table with two tall chairs.

"So, spill it! How was your day?" Anya asked as her beautiful blonde curls swept alongside her perfect face.

"Okay, I guess. My boss is kind of a jerk. It will turn out fine though, I'm sure," I said with hesitation and animosity in my voice.

I wasn't about divulging my feelings. I had a hard enough time as it was dealing with the shit I grew up with. Only a few people knew what my family and I went through. I'm sure if I was half-honest with Anya, she would understand why I had such a pessimistic view of the world. I wasn't trying to make excuses for myself, but if anyone had gone through what I did, I'm sure they would have been way more fucked up than I was.

We talked over a few bottles of red wine about my internship and her newest love interest, which changed from month to month. I did like hearing about her love life because mine was almost nonexistent, with the exception of a few drunken one-night stands I had throughout college and some library Harlequin novels I would regularly check out. It had been a dry spell for quite some time. I couldn't remember the last time I had been with a man.

I never had any close relationships with men. I had more of a tendency to push people away who tried to get close with me. I dated off and on in high school, but they were all bone-headed football players and jocks that hardly cared what my interests were. They just wanted me in bed, and most of the time, I surrendered to try to feel worthy—when in the end all it did was make me feel worse about myself. I never had a steady boyfriend in college, which was also a reflection of my disruptive view on love. There was just the *problem*.

After one too many glasses of wine, Anya had convinced me to follow her to the small dance area that was located next to the stage where the woman pianist was playing and singing in her beautiful alto voice. Anya was ready to show the men in the bar what she had. I, on the other hand, didn't have much to show. At least that was how I felt.

We started dancing slowly to the woman pianist's sexy voice. She was singing a variety of tunes. She started vocalizing Joss Stone's "4 and 20." I loved her music and let myself go along to the lovely, sultry piano tune. I was swaying my hips back and forth, my eyes closed, praying to return to my happy place for a moment or two.

As the song ended, I started feeling a little self-conscious and decided to head back to our little table in the corner and top off my wine. Anya remained on the dance floor. She had no worries. She was the most confident person I knew. I wish I could feel that, if only for a few seconds.

I noticed a table of attractive businessmen, and one in particular caught my attention. I didn't want to stare but found it hard to resist. He was a beautiful man and one that I would probably never see again. I would certainly not have the courage to exchange words with him. Men like that never seemed too interested in me. A girl could dream.

After distracting myself from the gorgeous man, I finished off my wine and decided to call it a night. I walked onto the small dance area where Anya was still moving her hips, continuing to watch most of the men in the bar swoon over her.

I hugged her good-bye and told her I would take a cab home. I pledged to text or call her in the morning, which I would try my best to remember. I did well enough remembering to call my mom on a weekly basis to play catch up.

I waved down a cab and noticed the same man I eyed from the bar. I tried not to look over at his GQ-like body, but fuck … it was difficult. He was six foot something, well built, and appeared to be in his mid to late twenties with dark brown hair and scruff on his face. He looked at me with piercing emerald green eyes. His lips were full, plush, and the perfect color of pink. I found my mind wondering what his kiss would taste like, and a hello from him brought me back to reality.

"Where to?" Mr. Gorgeous asked me.

I was dumbstruck that he was interested in where I was going. I stood there for a few moments trying to gather my thoughts and finally replied, "South Michigan Avenue, Azul Towers."

"I just moved there! Want to share a cab?" he asked with hope in his eyes.

"Sure," I replied, trying not to slur my words.

As we entered the cab, I felt an energy I had never sensed before. It could've been the red wine, but I don't think I had ever been as confident in my life. We observed one other at the same instant. He smiled at me, showing off his perfect model smile, which made his whole face light up like the ball that dropped in Times Square on New Year's Eve.

I tried to bring myself back to reality to convince myself that there was no way in hell he would ever be interested in a girl like me. I could wish.

The cabbie stopped at my apartment tower, and the handsome man insisted on paying the fare. I didn't complain or say anything. I was stunned that this lovely man was sitting next to me, one who was now living in my apartment building and acting half-interested in me.

Beer boner, I said to myself in my buzzing brain.

Men like that didn't care for a girl like me, all fucked up in the head. I was sure it showed on the outside. Maybe that was why I had never fallen in love. I wasn't sure I ever would. I had always wanted to but was positive there was no man out there who could handle all the baggage. I was not sure if I was interested in sharing it either.

"What's your name?" he said with a half smirk.

"Lyla, Lyla Harper," I answered, stuttering my words.

How embarrassing. I couldn't even start a conversation off right. I felt the perspiration on my brow, and my lips trembled. My legs started to tingle. *Stop now, Lyla … fucking compose yourself.*

"Nice to meet you," he answered with his hand extended. "My name is Everett Brown." I shook his strong hand, wondering what it would feel like if it held me. I wondered if he detected that my palms were sweaty. I was sure he recognized my anxiety. I was pretty certain at that point that my jet-black eyeliner was starting to smudge down my face from the sweat.

"I noticed you in the bar. I was hoping you would come talk to me," he said.

Wow, the beauty had a name. I was sure that was a face and name I would never forget. He had to be joking; there was absolutely no way that a man like him hoped for me to talk with him at the bar. Oh well. I came up with the courage and asked, "Want to come up for a drink? I live in 1002. Where is your apartment?"

"I live in 4024, and yes I would love to have a drink with you" he said with joy in his voice.

I had never been this lucky. I knew that men found me attractive in an exotic kind of way (at least that's what they would say when they were drunk at the bar with only pussy on their minds). I was the type of girl that was a magnet for one-night stands. Men must have used me as their last resort, decent enough looking and obviously vulnerable with no self-esteem. Check! It was part of the messed-up shit that had been drilled in my head for so many years. Counseling sure never fixed that part of me.

And he lived in the penthouse suite? Oh. My. God. My little one-bedroom apartment wouldn't have anything on his penthouse, but I didn't care … that must have been the alcohol.

We hopped into the elevator, me slightly stumbling. It was apparent that I had one too many glasses of shiraz. That had to be it. That had to be why he agreed (light bulb on again ... vulnerable Lyla with a gorgeous man next to her with sex on his mind. Easy for him to settle for a girl like me).

I was sure it would turn into a quick fuck and then would be over with. I would then run into him in the elevator and be mortified. Oh well, I didn't feel like being careful. It was a risk I was willing to take, and I hadn't taken any risks in quite some time. That was a problem for me. Was I turning back into the darkness? Shredding more pieces of my life? I didn't care. I was ready for a drink with Everett Brown.

Chapter 3

I FISHED FOR my keys in my purse. After what seemed like forever with his handsome face staring over at me, I found them and put them in the door and unlocked it. Trying to walk without tripping in my red pumps, I entered my apartment with slight embarrassment. I had forgotten to pick up before leaving that morning, which was something I almost never overlooked. Go figure that on the night I bring Mr. Beautiful into my apartment, it was disheveled.

"Come in, please. I'll just be a minute. Would you prefer shiraz or cabernet sauvignon?" I asked, trying to sound confident like I was some kind of ritzy wine aficionado. I knew he was higher class than I was, considering his living arrangement in the penthouse suite and his three-piece Prada suit.

"Either would be great. I love red wine," he responded, penetrating me with those amazing green eyes. His eyes reminded me of the greenest of grass … the kind that carpets the hills of beautiful Ireland.

I picked up a few items, put them back into their places, and poured two glasses of red cabernet into two of my favorite stemless wine glasses. I made my way over to my couch and sat next to him, offering his glass to him.

He swirled the glass around, sniffed the contents, took a small sip, swishing it in his mouth, and then swallowed. He proceeded to smile. My eyes were stuck on that heavenly Adam's apple on his stubbly throat. *Ah! Stop it, Lyla!* I hoped he didn't notice me gawking at his throat, but that had to have been the sexiest thing I had ever seen a man do. Wow.

"Thank you. You have a nice place. So what do you do?" he asked.

"I just completed my last semester at Loyola, public relations and marketing. Just started at an advertising firm as an intern. What do you do?" I responded, trying to compose myself.

"Just finished up law school. Recently started at Boyd, Lewis & Schmidt." Wow, not only was he stunningly gorgeous but also intelligent. There had to be a catch.

"Do you like music?" he asked.

"Yeah, all kinds," I said.

He pulled out his iPhone and plugged it into my iDock sitting on the coffee table. He took some time scrolling down his phone with his long—and I was sure talented—fingers, as if he were trying to find the best song to play. Moments later, the melancholy tune started, and the amazing lyrics of "Breathe Me" by Sia buzzed elegantly from the tiny speakers on my second-hand, vintage, tiled coffee table.

My heart dropped to the floor, my lungs started to sting, and I lost my breath. *Breathe now, Lyla!* That was one of my much-loved songs. I felt as though the lyrics were written for me. I fought to continue my shallow breaths and keep my anxiety hidden as he took my hand into his. I hadn't battled with my anxiety that much since leaving Rigdon four years before.

His grip was gentle but masculine as he took my hand into his.

"Dance with me," he said, pulling me to my feet. God, even his voice got to me.

I grabbed his hand and together we danced as he occasionally sang with his lips brushing against my ear. "Be my friend, hold me, wrap me up, unfold me ..." My heart and soul were melting. I wanted to slap myself and wake up from what felt like a dream. I felt my body reacting in a way that I thought was damaged forever.

I was getting aroused by his everything. Butterflies swarmed in my belly, and I felt my heart flutter. Even though I had been with a few men after my *problem*, none had the same effect on me as Everett Brown. I was confused. I didn't understand why he was so different from the rest. I wanted to know more. It was the first time I ever really cared about getting to know a man.

His right hand was intertwined with my left, and his left hand rested softly on my lower back in the perfect place within my curves. It felt as if his hands belonged to me. I tried so hard not to lay my head on his shoulder, but my body could not resist it. It felt right. My right arm was draped snuggly over his neck, and our bodies were lost in dance.

I knew my soul was ripping open again. It scared me. I didn't want to get hurt again. I couldn't handle it. My brain would burst, and I would end up in another sinking helix, unsure if I could get through one more.

But I couldn't stop; I was willing to take the gamble. Life was worth one more chance, even if only for one night. No questions asked ... this man dancing with me at this moment had to be heaven sent ... possibly an angel himself. But again, I didn't know why!

It seemed like forever that we were dancing in each other's arms, and I didn't want the song to end, but it did.

He looked down at me and said, "Has anyone ever told you how utterly beautiful you are?"

I was shocked. I couldn't find the words to express how flabbergasted I was. I did not reply. *Say something … anything, Lyla! Don't fuck this up!*

"You must get that a lot. Am I making you uncomfortable? Should I leave?"

I grabbed his face with his stubble tickling the palms of my hands and brought it to mine. His full, perfect, pink lips met my welcoming mouth, and we kissed with magic and tenderness, our tongues sweeping against each other's. I was in heaven, and I never wanted that second to cease.

"Wow," he exclaimed as our first kiss ended. I was ready for more, no doubt about that.

He looked down at me as if he were trying to gather my thoughts. I felt something. I wasn't sure what it was or if I could handle it, but there was no way in hell I was going to let it go. Was I crazy for thinking that Everett Brown would be my saving grace? Could he guard me from myself? What about this man made me have these unfamiliar thoughts? I was scared, insecure, unsure, but I needed him.

I smiled at him—not the usual fake smile, but a smile that was real. A smile that was full of delight and promise. I was showing him that I was truly happy in the moments he had given me.

He reached over and took my ponytail down. My long, black, curly hair tumbled down my back to just a few inches above my bottom. He ran his strong hands through my hair and then picked me up. I wrapped my long legs around his trim waist.

The next thing I knew, I was on my back on top of my queen-sized bed. He stood there for a twinkling, looking at me. Admiring *me*. I felt like the most gorgeous woman in the world. He made me feel that way, but I didn't know why.

He leaned over me, planting a sweet kiss on my forehead, looking into my soul with those emerald eyes. I took his face with passion, and our lips met again. Our tongues were lost in each other's, twirling perfectly to our own rhythm.

He unbuttoned my blouse and took it off. That was a first for me. No other man, besides my *problem* that I left in Rigdon, had seen me completely naked in the light. I was sitting on the bed in my lacy pink bra with my God-given Ds pouring over and hard-as-rock nipples trying to push their way out. I then realized that my imperfect stomach was staring straight at him.

Something in the air had changed. The self-consciousness had resurfaced, and I felt a pain in my gut, an aching from the past that I thought I could forget when I was in his embrace.

I pushed him off of me with tears filling my eyes. I knew he saw the scars that looked like roadmaps on my abdomen. He stood quickly and moved away from me with his head hanging, not knowing what to say.

"I'm so sorry. I just don't think I can do this," I said with tears streaming down my face.

"Did I do something?" he replied, looking back up at me, perplexed as if he hadn't seen the scars.

I knew he did. They were hard to miss. They were a constant reminder of my past. Forever I would be reminded of why I was so fucked up. And I was fucked up again, on Everett Brown.

"Please, go. I'm sorry again. This shouldn't have happened. Just forget about me."

"Lyla, I don't know what I did. If I made you feel—"

"Stop. Please," I interrupted. "Just go. I'm sure you'll forget about me by the time your feet hit the doormat."

"Lyla, please. I'm sorry. Don't do this. Can I stay so we can talk?"

"No, Everett, it's best if you go. You don't know what you're getting yourself into. And besides, I'm sure you had no intention of getting to know me. You just wanted a piece of ass. Good-bye."

I didn't give him a chance to respond. I opened the front door with my eyes looking down. I knew if our eyes met again, I would cry harder. He walked out with less elegance than when he strolled in. I heard his echoing footsteps finally fade away. I crawled into my bed and cried myself to sleep.

Chapter 4

I AWOKE TO my buzzing alarm clock, regretting what had happened the night before. My head was pounding from too much wine and crying. I stepped out of my bed and saw my blouse lying on the floor, looking down with the thoughts that had troubled me from the night before.

I got into the shower and felt the all too familiar tears flood my eyes. I couldn't stop crying. Why? I thought. He was a guy that I knew for a few hours. Why was I crying over him? I was being ridiculous.

"Get over it, Lyla," I said to myself out loud.

I got out of the shower, taking extra precaution not to look at my naked body in the mirror. That would just make things worse.

I went into my bedroom closet and chose my outfit for the day. I donned my new black suit pants and put on a light blue blouse and matching black suit jacket. I then chose some black peep-toe wedges to complete my outfit.

I decided to wear my hair down. It took forever to straighten since I had natural curl, but I was willing to take the time to try to make myself feel better. I put some concealer underneath my eyes to hide the dark circles, and I put a small amount of blush, mascara, and clear lip gloss on. I grabbed my mother's pearl studs out of my jewelry cabinet and placed them in my ears and then grabbed my purse and keys.

I didn't want to be late; it wasn't in my nature, and being on time consisted of being fifteen minutes early. As I stepped out of my apartment, I felt a crinkle underneath my shoe. There was a white envelope that had *Lyla* written elegantly on the front. I opened it, and it was a note from him. A handwritten note from Everett Brown.

Lyla,

I'm not sure what happened last night. Can we put it behind us and start over? I would really like to have the opportunity to get to know you better. Please call.

Everett

Shit. What was I supposed to do? Sorry for freaking out because I have scars covering my stomach? Sorry for having a fucked-up past that has consumed me and prevented me from feeling an ounce of true contentment? Sorry that I made those scars? Who would ever be able to understand?

I knew someone who I could talk to that would give me a better perspective on the situation that I was more than likely over analyzing. I picked up my cell and called my sister, Rosalynn. She wasn't only my sister, but also my best friend. The six-year age gap meant nothing. She was six when I was born, and we had been close ever since.

"Hello?" said Rosalynn.

"Hey, Ros."

"What's going on, Lyla? Are you all right?"

"Well, maybe not …"

Over the course of my twenty-minute drive, I filled her in about last night's drama.

"Lyla, you can't continue to give up every time something good comes your way. You're a good person. Others see it too; you just have to learn to see it in yourself. Call him for goodness sake. He sounds hot, smart, and caring. And even if it doesn't work out or nothing comes from it, it's a lesson learned."

"Thanks, Rosalynn. You always have a way of making me feel better. How are Aidan and the boys?"

"Keeping me busy. I feel like I'm running around half-crazy sometimes, but I just love the life we have here! Thankfully, Aidan only sees patients in the office now. He has the hospitalists take his patients on if they're admitted to the hospital."

She was a former nurse who stayed at home with her two boys, age two and five. Her husband was an internal medicine physician. They had met when he was doing rounds in the ICU at the hospital and had been inseparable ever since. He was a good man, worthy to my sister, and I was grateful for that.

I arrived at the office fifteen minutes before nine. I reached my work area, remembering what Mr. Pervert Asshole expected of me every morning. I went into the break room and prepared his coffee as he liked it. When I returned, he was already sitting in his throne with displeasure and anger written all over his face. I walked into his office with his coffee and went to set it on his desk.

"Sit, now," said Mr. Thomas.

I did what I was told and sat directly across from him. "Did you forget my list of expectations, Miss Harper?"

"I'm sorry, Mr. Thomas. I got your coffee as you like it …"

"I'm talking about your wardrobe choice. Why the fuck are you wearing pants? Was I not clear enough on what you were to wear?"

I was in complete disbelief. This was obviously sexual harassment. Who would believe me? A Midwestern girl from a shitty town who moved to Chicago to try to become successful or a multi-million-dollar fucker who managed the most successful public relations and marketing firms?

I had no choice but to obey this asshole and hope that it would get better. I couldn't quit. I wasn't going to allow him to get to me. I wanted to prove to the professional world that I was worth something.

"This is strike one, Miss Harper. You are on thin ice right now. I highly recommend that this not happen again, understood? And another coffee please; this one is cold."

Fuck you, I said to myself in my head as I smiled back at him with a nod. I went and got him another and sat it on his desk, hoping I was breathing right. I didn't want to get fired; I just wanted to get through this internship. It was going to be helpful on my resume, and I wasn't about to give that up.

I checked his schedule and noticed he had no lunches planned. I looked at his preferred restaurant choices and chose an Italian bistro that was close by. I sifted through their menu and called ahead to preorder his food at the bistro so it was ready by the time I got there.

I didn't want to be late returning his meal to him. I didn't want strike two. I must have done that right because he didn't scold me the rest of the day. He left me alone for the most part, sitting on his throne like he was the king of his castle.

I looked up at the clock and saw that it was a few minutes until five. I gathered my things, thankful that it was Friday and that I would have two days away from that prick. I double-checked the schedule for Monday, trying to stay on top of my game before I got strike two. I was about to step out of my tiny cubicle, and he was standing there, grinning at me like I was some fucking prize.

"It's not five o'clock yet," he said.

One gosh-damn minute before five, and I wasn't allowed to leave? What the fuck was this control freak about? I had too much on my plate to deal with his shit. He sat there staring at me, looking my body up and down as if he were undressing me with his eyes. It brought back memories of my *problem* I left back in Rigdon, Kansas. I was disgusted but tried not to show it. One minute felt like forever.

"You may go, Miss Harper" he said in an obvious sexual tone.

As I turned to walk away, I felt his hand grope my backside.

"Nice ass, sweetie," he said.

I wanted to slap him, run away, and never come back. But I didn't want to give up so easily, without a fight. I left Rigdon without a fight, and I wasn't about to do the same here in Chicago. I was going to fight for the happiness I deserved and establish my place in this fucked-up world.

I made my way to the parking garage and my car, thinking through what had happened the past few days. Dreamy man, check. Prick boss, check. Self-medicating through wine, check. What was I going to do with myself?

I pulled out the note from my purse, contemplating dialing Everett's number. I wanted to summon the courage to call him. I figured I would wait until I got home. As I walked up to my apartment, I was hoping I wouldn't run into Mr. Perfect. Thankfully I didn't.

I entered my apartment and stepped onto my balcony, lighting the first of many cigarettes and trying to figure out what to do. I decided to grab a beer from the fridge; after all, I was a pro at self-soothing to cover up how I was feeling, to mask the hurt.

After two beers without a buzz, I grabbed my cell phone, staring at his number. I punched the digits into my iPhone with The Oh Hello's "Hello My Old Heart" playing in the background. I pressed call ... and then hung up after the first ring. Gosh, why was I being such a coward? Was I that scared of facing my past again? Would he help me trust again? I decided to take the chance and call again. He answered on the first ring.

"Hello?" his perfect voice said.

"Everett?" I said.

"Lyla, I'm so glad you decided to call. Can we meet to talk? Just a friendly conversation. I promise nothing more."

"Sure. Where do you want to meet?"

"Is your apartment okay again or would you like to go to dinner?" I sure as hell didn't feel like being around a lot of people, so I agreed to meet at my place.

He arrived looking even more gorgeous than I remembered. He was dressed in jeans that hung perfectly around his trim and fit waist with a T-shirt that clung to his muscular build. I found myself undressing him with my eyes, wondering how he would feel in bed with me.

"Come in, please," I said, embarrassed.

"Lyla, I'm so glad that you agreed to meet. I'm not sure what happened last night, but let's just forget about it and start over. I'm Everett Brown," he said with his hand out to me.

I smiled at him and shook his hand. I felt the familiar feeling of the thunderbolt of energy rush through my body. I only felt that when we touched. I started to tingle in places that I thought were damaged forever.

"Nice to meet you, Everett. I'm Lyla Harper," I said flirtatiously. "So, Everett, tell me a little bit about yourself," I said, gesturing for him to sit on my faux suede couch.

"Well, I'm a lawyer, like I mentioned. I specialize in criminal law. I grew up outside of Chicago near the Gold Coast. Do you know where that is?" he asked.

I nodded to him, not at all shocked. The Gold Coast was a rich suburb of Chicago. Aston Martins, Ducatis, prep-schools, and

European vacations were the normal part of growing up near The Gold Coast.

"My dad died when I was only two," he said. "It was a car wreck. A drunk driver ran a red light and hit him head on. He died instantly, but the driver walked away without a scratch. I don't remember much about him."

I felt as if it was my turn to share something personal with him. Even though he had been a young child, it had to be painful to talk about. I understood all about loss, even though my situation was much different from his.

"I understand what it's like to lose a parent. My dad died when I was six years old," I said without giving him details. I was hoping he would not ask.

"Your turn to answer some questions," he said coyly.

"Oh, okay," I said with slight hesitancy in my voice.

"What are your dreams?" he asked.

I was not even remotely sure how to answer that request. I wanted to tell him so badly that I wished to learn to live life happily. To put the past in the past and keep it there. I wanted a promise that it would never resurface and cause me any pain.

I could not share my thoughts and real dreams with him. It was too early, and he would not be able to understand. I would surely scare him away letting him know that. He wouldn't want to get involved with a girl like me.

"I, uh, I guess to become a successful business woman," I replied.

Safe enough answer, I thought.

"Where are you originally from?" he pressed.

It was apparent that this man was trying to get to know me more than any other guy I had brought to my apartment. Wait, he was the first man who ever attempted to dive deeper than the periphery. I was stunned, and as much as I wanted to give up all my skeletons, I hastened myself.

"Rigdon, Kansas … a very tiny town."

"What brought you to Chicago?" he asked.

"School. Like I said the other night, I just graduated from Loyola."

Okay, he was definitely going to continue to press me for personal questions. I had to change the subject and take charge of the evening.

"My turn," I said, shooting him a smile. "Any brothers or sisters?" I asked.

"My brother, Rowan, is twenty-eight. He's also an attorney. He specializes in real estate law. He lives in New York City. Married with a kid … he has the whole gig," he answered with a smirk.

The whole gig? Is this something that he wanted in life? I never brought myself to think about marriage and children. I could barely take care of myself. After all, no one had ever tried taking care of me. Who knows, maybe one day some man would want to. Maybe Everett? *No, Lyla! Stop getting ahead of yourself!*

We continued conversing on my couch, discussing everything from the weather to Wall Street, politics, and our outlook on religion. He had a passion for reading and music, and he played the guitar well. I was even more surprised to learn he grew up Catholic like I did. We did have a lot in common. As the evening progressed, I became more comfortable in his presence and more secure in myself.

We listened to music as we did the night before, and I promised myself to try not to screw it up like I had formerly. Kate Nash's "Nicest Thing" started playing. We held each other as our bodies did the rest, moving to the music. He reached down to the nape of my neck and kissed me smoothly. I was in heaven again.

We moved back into my bedroom, kissing each other along the way. I felt the back of my knees hit the bed. He gently laid me down on the bed so that I was lying on my back. He then proceeded to remove my shirt with kindness. I tried not to cringe or be embarrassed. I refused to let my past ruin something good again.

His skillful fingers unclasped my bra, and my full breasts bounced free into his wondrous hands. His fingers lightly caressed my nipples, sending an incredible feeling throughout my body. His mouth made its way to one of my breasts as he sucked one of my nipples, making my body on high alert. I wanted him, and I needed him now.

"You are absolute heaven, Lyla, perfect in every way possible."

I didn't need to say anything. I responded by a lengthy and ardent kiss. He touched my stomach. His beautiful face made its way down to my stomach as he started kissing every scar. My hands were holding onto his dark mane.

It felt as if his tender kisses were curing me. Taking the agony away with every single one of his traces and feather-light kisses. His lips felt perfect on my damaged skin.

He took his shirt off, showing off his dreamily sculpted chest and stomach. I ran my hands down his pectorals and abs and stopped at his fly to his pants. I popped it open and pulled his pants down. He wasn't wearing underwear, which was erotic as hell. He spread my legs open, and I welcomed him for another adoring kiss. I yearned for him to rip my panties off ... I was ready to do it myself. His marvelous hands made their way down to my hips, and on both sides he grasped my underwear and took them off with pure grace.

He climbed on top of me, spreading my legs apart, searching my eyes to make sure I was still okay with what was happening ...

man oh man, I was way more than okay with it. I responded by bucking my hips so my wet, wanting heat grinded against his erection.

He hadn't entered me yet. He was taking his sweet time. He was a delectable morsel of a man and soul. If I could feel this way forever. I would, no doubt about that.

Our chests were skin to skin, and the feeling was of pure ecstasy. He looked into my eyes and into my soul. I knew it was a first for me, feeling that way with a man ... confident, sexy, secure, and loved. He entered me, and I was sure at that moment that the Fourth of July had nothing on us.

He was gentle, making love to me with slow strokes of perfection. He cupped my face, kissing me passionately, and as our lips released, our eyes met. I felt the unfamiliar sensation of the impending orgasm building up in my body. I wanted to let go so badly, but I continued to hold back.

I closed my eyes, fighting the explosion that was impending within my body. I stopped breathing and could feel my lungs feel like they were on fire. *Stop it*, I said to myself, but I couldn't let it go. I was scared to experience one after the last one I had ... when I was eighteen, young and naïve. Tears started to pool in my eyes as I opened them to meet his. It was as if he could read my mind; he knew I was holding back.

"Let it go, Lyla ... let me feel you come," he whispered as he dug deeper into my pelvis, hitting the right spot while gently tugging on my erect nipple.

With those words, I allowed myself to let go, my body shaking uncontrollably and my voice screaming out incoherently. His strokes became harder and harder, and I felt another one coming on.

"Please, Everett" I panted, pleading with him to make me come again.

"Come with me, baby," he said as his expert fingers rubbed my swollen clit.

"God, ah, please come in me, please, Everett," I pleaded.

My muscles ached and clenched around his swollen cock, releasing my fluids that were now dripping down the crack of my ass.

"Fuck.You. Feel. So. Damn. Good." He shuddered as his body grew rigid, and his eyes closed as he enjoyed his release into me.

That was the first orgasm I had experienced since the one that was forced upon me when I was eighteen, scared, alone, and lost in the middle of the woods in Rigdon, Kansas, with my *problem*.

He collapsed on top of me. I rubbed his perfect back and kissed his shoulder. That was beyond intense, and I was sure that I wanted to feel all of that again. It was mutual, not forced. I felt safe in his embrace. Hell would freeze over before I let this man out of my life. I was determined not to fuck it up.

As the night went on, we made love over and over again. That was the first time I had ever made love to a man. He was the first man to see me naked in the light, the first to recognize my past.

As we lay next to each other, our unclothed bodies spooned like perfect puzzle pieces, he stroked my stomach, like he knew it was therapeutic. As if he was reassuring me that it was okay, no matter how they happened. I knew I didn't have to give details until I was ready. And I discerned I wouldn't be equipped anytime soon.

I wanted to relish this night like it was my last to live. I wanted to stay in his hold forever. I was falling in love with Everett Brown. I never believed in love at first sight until I laid my eyes on him. I knew it was spot on.

Chapter 5

I WOKE UP to his warm, even breaths on my neck. Our bodies still clung together like we were meant to be that way. I determined I wasn't the only one who felt that. I could see it in him too. The way he looked at me when we made love. It felt as if our eyes were meant for each other's gaze.

"Good morning, beautiful," he said with a huge grin. He kissed me on my cheek.

"Good morning, Everett. Hungry? Want me to cook something for you?"

"I'm not hungry for any food, just for you."

I was in a complete trance. He positioned his hands on the sides of my face, looking at me, tantalizing me with those eyes. His full lips met mine, and our tongues moved to our own pace. Our bodies were reacting to each other's.

I got aroused just by looking at the god of the man that was sharing my bed with me. He had to have been heaven sent; he sure seemed like an angel to me. He touched every inch of my body, exploring it like no one ever had before, and I loved it.

He gently rolled me over so I was on top of him. "I like you like this, so I can see all of you," he said.

I leaned up so he could place his large cock inside me. The feeling was overwhelming and very sensitive. I had never had sex like this before, on top of a man willingly, and naked from the top up.

The fullness became more comfortable for me, and I was strained to my maximum. He placed his hand on the bottom of my belly near my womb and said, "I can feel myself inside you. It's perfect."

His words tipped me over the edge, and I let my body go, succumbing to an intense and emotional orgasm, spilling myself around him. I wasn't sure how, but my body continued its rhythm, back and forth, up and down. I wanted him to let himself go inside me as well.

"Fuck," he huffed as he poured himself into my wet pussy.

I slumped over him with his half-rigid cock still inside me. He held me, and I was sure there was no place that I ever wanted to be more than in his embrace. I finally looked up at him through my honey brown eyes, resting my chin on his perfectly chiseled chest. I smirked at him.

I was proud of myself that a girl like me could have such an effect on a man like him. I was sure I didn't deserve him. He seemed too good to be true. I needed to know why he was so attracted to me. I was clearly fucked up physically and emotionally. I couldn't hide it from him, and he hadn't hit the ground yet.

Why was he like a moth to a flame with me? It was obvious why I was to him; he was handsome, kind, nonjudgmental, accepting … the list was endless. But I needed to figure out why he wanted a girl like me. I was sure he could have anyone he wanted, yet he chose me. I had to know, but not now. I wanted to relish the time we were spending together.

"I couldn't have asked for a better morning," he said, smiling from ear to ear.

"Ditto," I said, smiling like I never have before.

I rolled over and lay next to him. He rubbed my ribs, caressing my tattoo.

"I love all your tattoos," he said.

"Really? Even though you don't have any? Most people are so disapproving of them," I stated.

"What's the one between your shoulders?" he asked while rubbing it with his expert fingers.

"My favorite! It says *Only God Can Judge Me* in Hebrew."

"I love it. I think they're sexy, especially on your perfect skin."

"You mean my imperfect skin? Never mind that."

He knew better than to ask my about my statement. I did not want to open up that can of worms, at least not yet. I had to find out why he wanted and needed me. It didn't make sense. I was hoping that my insecurities didn't get the best of me. I didn't want to push him away. Was it wrong of me to want to know why he wanted a fucked-up girl like me even though I was nowhere near equipped to tell him about my skeletons that had stayed hidden in the closet for the past four years?

I dismissed my thoughts and focused my attention back on Everett. I would be satisfied to lay in bed all day and stare at this beautiful creature that God had decided to throw into my life.

We finally made our way out of bed, and I made him breakfast dressed in an oversized T-shirt and boy-cut underwear. I was making eggs on my stove.

"Don't move," he said slyly. "I want to remember this moment forever, the way you look. I've never seen anything else so striking in my life than you, Miss Lyla Harper."

I couldn't help but beam. The mode in which the words rolled of his tongue made me want to fall to my knees. Every muscle in my body went weak, but I felt my soul strengthening. He was restoring me with every gaze, every word, every kiss, and every touch. I was sure he was my saving grace, and I thanked God every second for putting him in my life. I wasn't sure where things would end up, but I was more than willing to go along for the ride.

After breakfast, we made our way to the bathroom. I started the shower and turned around and found him staring at me. I tried not to blush but felt the blood rushing to my cheeks.

"No need to be embarrassed, Lyla. Don't you recognize just how beautiful you are, all of you?"

He took two steps toward me, our mouths just inches apart. I felt his sweet breath on my lips. His hands made their way to my hips to the edge of my T-shirt. He lifted it off of me. I was standing in front of him in only my underwear.

He kissed me avidly, sweetly, lovingly. Our tongues danced in marvelous tune. As he finished undressing me, he lifted me up, and I wrapped my legs around his waist with my feet resting in the perfect place above his ass. We burst into the shower, making love again.

I knew I could never get enough of him. He made me feel so good, like I was a woman worth something.

"You feel amazing. This is perfect," he said, panting as he poured his seed into my body.

We decided to lounge around lazily after our shower. We continued to converse about nothing in depth. As the day went on, he revealed more about his life than I was willing to about mine. It was obvious that I was dodging some issues.

"Tell me more about yourself, Everett. I want to know everything about you," I said.

"Well, my mother, Marie, remarried when I was ten. The guy is an ass, always has been and always will be. But he gives my mother whatever she desires. My mother is a good woman, but after my father died, and she met my stepdad, she materialized life.

"My stepdad made sure to send us to boarding schools and make us travel abroad in the summers so he could have Mother all to himself. Don't get me wrong, my brother and I never wanted for anything. But if I have learned anything in my twenty-six years of life, it's not the things that matter the most. It's the people you meet, the encounters you experience, and the life you learn. That's what's most important."

I found myself smiling from ear to ear. It was nice to hear something so sweet. Most rich people I'd met seemed to covet money and their assets, my boss being one of them. Flashing his money in his throne of an office.

"Tell me about your family," he said inquisitively.

"My mother's name is Marguerite. Her parents were from Sicily and migrated to the States when my mom was a baby. My mom and dad married, and my sister was born ten months later. Her name is Rosalynn. She's my best friend. She's married with two kids. My brother, Garret, is two years older than me. He fought the war in Iraq as a marine.

"Rick is my stepdad. Mom remarried when I was twelve. He's basically like a dad to me. Like I told you before, my dad died when I was six. I grew up in the country, and we went on camping trips a lot. I have some fond memories of my family, though I haven't been home in four years ..." I trailed off.

I had to stop myself before I got in too deep. I wasn't ready to reveal anything past that. But how could I avoid the unavoidable? Surely any normal person would wonder why an individual who appeared so close to their family hadn't returned to their hometown in four years.

"I've been pretty busy the past four years with college and working. Around holidays, my family comes here to visit me. Sometimes we meet halfway for a brief visit," I said, trying to convince him.

He eyed me with skepticism. I couldn't blame him. I would too. I started to get the all too familiar sensation of tingling in my limbs. I started sweating, and my heart was racing. I tried to take a few deep breaths to calm myself before the inevitable anxiety attack; that was a true part of me.

"Excuse me," I said as I darted into the bathroom and locked the door behind me.

I slid down the bathroom door, avoiding the mirror, which always made the anxiety attacks worse. Seeing my unworthy face … bringing back all the bad memories. I held my head in my sweaty hands.

Count to ten, Lyla … one, two, three, four. Deep breath. *Five, six, seven, eight, nine, ten. Breathe. Compose yourself, Lyla!* I shouted to myself in my bustling brain.

A soft knock came from my bathroom door.

"Lyla? Are you okay? Let's find a movie on demand. We can veg out on the couch the rest of the day. How does that sound?"

God answered my prayers. Everett must have known that I had secrets I wasn't ready to tell him, and he was willing to accept that. I got my panic under control by splashing cool water on my face, still avoiding the mirror, taking a few more deep breaths, and finally composing myself enough. I opened the door, and he greeted me with a sincere smile.

"Sounds excellent," I said with sincerity.

We snuggled on the couch, and he assured me that I could pick out any movie I wanted. I went with *The Godfather.* It was a classic, and I knew that most men loved that movie. I loved that movie as well. It had to be the Sicilian in my blood.

We spooned on my couch, and before I knew it, I dozed off into the arms of the man that I was falling in love with but hardly knew.

I woke up, and Everett was staring at me, smiling.

"Hungry?" he asked.

"Famished," I replied. I hadn't eaten much that day (even though I was sure I could stand to lose some weight).

"How does Chinese takeout sound?"

"Perfect," I replied.

Thirty minutes later, we sat in my living room eating sweet and sour chicken and spring rolls. We topped our meal off with a few Heinekens while watching *The League*. It was a man's show, but I found myself laughing hysterically. It was the best day I had had in a really long time. I needed it.

"Tell me about where you grew up," he said before stuffing another spring roll into his perfect mouth.

"Well, I grew up in Rigdon, Kansas. It's the kind of place where everyone knows everything about one another. Hunting, fishing, football games, and bonfires were always the most important things in town. Most people who grow up there never leave. They always end up marrying their high school sweetheart, and the vicious cycle continues."

"How did you escape that?" he asked.

"I was determined to get out. I had college scholarships. I don't really want to go there," I said with discontent in my voice. I knew he was trying to dig deeper, but I wasn't ready for it.

"I'm sorry, Lyla. I didn't mean to offend you."

"It's okay. There's just a lot I'm not ready to talk about. Like I said the other night, I'm fucked up. I'm used to scaring people off and pushing people away when things get tough. I want things to be different with you, Everett."

He never asked another question about why I left home. I knew he would wait until I was ready to open up. But I wasn't sure how to tell him all the twisted shit that happened to me. I didn't want pity; after all, a lot of it was my doing. At least that was my view on it. The *problem* was how I referred to it. That was what it was. One big fucking problem that changed my life forever.

Chapter 6

THE FOLLOWING WEEK, Everett made plans to take me out on a real date. I was beyond delighted! The past week, we had been doing nothing but hanging out at each other's places, watching movies, and having lots and lots of hot sex. Don't get me wrong, I was in heaven, but I had never been out on a real date before. I was excited.

I showered and washed my body. It was a first for me, not to feel the tears pool in my eyes as I washed my scarred stomach. I was hoping to put the past in the past and keep it there. Bury it in a very deep, dark hole and never revisit it.

I stepped out of the shower and wrapped a towel around my body. I walked into my bedroom and opened my closet, trying to decide what to wear. I wanted to make him hard the moment he saw me. I decided to go with a strapless, black cocktail dress that fell just above my knees. I donned my black pumps and went light on the makeup. I applied a small amount of concealer under my eyes, pale pink lip gloss, and a bit of mascara to brighten up my eyes.

I grabbed my silver clutch and put my keys, phone, and cigs in there and walked out of my apartment to head up to the twentieth floor. To Everett's penthouse suite. It was beyond nice. I gave the door a few quiet knocks, and he opened the door. My jaw dropped to the floor!

He was wearing a black suit (which I was sure was Prada) with a crimson tie. I noticed his silver (probably platinum) cufflinks and his perfect shoes. His hair was wild, mussed, and still slightly wet from his shower.

"Like what you see, sweetheart?" he asked.

"Oh, yes," I responded. The self-consciousness was still lurking over me, but not as much as it typically had before I met Everett. I wasn't sure why. I still hadn't figured out why he wanted to be with a girl like me. I decided that tonight I would come out and ask him. I had to know. There had to be a reason why. Whether it was a good or bad thing, I deserved to know. Especially before I invested too much more time into our relationship. Was that what it was? A relationship?

I dismissed the thoughts and wrapped my arm around his. We headed toward the elevator, and as soon as the ding sounded, we entered it. Complete silence. I was getting nervous. I wasn't sure what I was supposed to do or say. I started to tremble.

"Lyla, my love, it's okay," he said.

"Sorry," I said, looking down at my black pumps.

"No reason to be sorry, love. I want to give you an evening to remember," he replied.

I smiled to myself, still looking down. It was out of habit. I was insecure. It was obvious.

He waved down a taxi and opened the door for me. I slid over, and he entered after me. I looked out the window, wondering what his plans were for me. He rambled some directions off to the driver, and we were on our way.

Within minutes, we arrived at our destination. Even though I had been in Chicago for four years, I hadn't seen the whole city. I stepped out onto a cobblestone walkway, and a tiny restaurant was right in front of me. It was gorgeous and intimate, overlooking the lake. He took my hand and led me inside. Our table for two was situated next to the wall of windows that had a breathtaking view.

"We will have a bottle of the 2009 Guigal Cote-Rotie La Maouline," he said to the waiter confidently.

For fuck's sake, I had no idea what the hell that was but was positive it was very expensive. I always settled for a cheap bottle of Yellow Tail shiraz.

"Thank you for taking me here," I said shyly.

"Anything for you, Lyla," he said with sincerity.

The waiter brought out our wine, poured two glasses, and Everett did that thing again! He swirled the contents, smelled it, took a small sip, swished it in his heavenly mouth, and swallowed.

I again was fixated on that heavenly Adam's apple on his stubbly neck. Gah! How would I be able to contain myself through dinner without jumping over the table and ravaging him in the middle of this ritzy place?

I took a drink, and it was the best red wine I had ever tasted. The taste was magnificent and lingered on my tongue.

"Everett, I need to ask you something. I'm going to be frank, and I need to know before we go any further with this, uh ... well, whatever it is," I said, blushing, trying to summon the courage to ask him what I had been dying to all week.

"Anything, Lyla. Is everything okay?" he asked with concern in his voice.

"Yes, I'm fine. I just, well ... I need to know, why me?"

"What do you mean?" he asked.

"I mean why would you choose to be with a girl like *me*? It's pretty obvious, Everett. I've got some issues, and a man like you could have any woman you wanted. Why me? That's the only question I have for you, and I need an answer before we decide to go any further with this," I said, gesturing to the space between us.

He took a large gulp of wine and then took a deep breath,

"Lyla, have you always been so down on yourself?" he asked.

"Don't turn this around on me, Everett. I need to know. After that, I will, in time, tell you more about myself. But in the meantime, I have to know. Why me?"

He sighed and looked up at me.

"My whole life has been nothing but structure. Everything has been planned out for me. Where I would attend boarding school, summer vacations, sports, clubs, college, and even the law firm I work at. I've always lived in a structured world where all decisions were made for me. Life was boring. I was just going through the motions of life. I mean, I can't complain. I have a nice place, a great job, and all ..." He trailed off.

"Continue," I said.

"I knew when I saw you at the piano bar that you were someone special. I don't know what it was, but you struck a light in me that I had never felt before. I didn't know what the hell it was, but I wanted to know more. You intrigued me.

"After the first night at your apartment, I realized I wanted nothing more than to help you."

"So, let me get this straight. You knew from the first night that I was some sad, broken girl, and you wanted to help me? So this past week you've been helping me? Fucking me to make me feel better about myself? Am I some charity case for you, Everett? A little adventure for you so that you strayed from your fucking structured world?" I said, with tears in my eyes.

I didn't want to make a scene. I simply got up and walked out of the restaurant. My pace grew faster, and I started to run. My pumps caught on the cobblestone, and I fell straight on my face, busting my lips.

I was crying uncontrollably and tasting the blood in the process. I got up and tried to run but felt a strong set of arms wrap around my body. It was Everett, my saving grace.

Chapter 7

"STOP, LYLA ... NOW. You are safe. Stop it," he chanted into my ear.

"I don't want to be some damn adventure for you, Everett. I don't want you to try and fix me! Is that what all this has been about? Fuck a sorry girl, make her feel better about herself? When were you planning on ending it?" I asked.

"Never," he said sternly.

He turned me around and kissed me, battered lips and all. Our mouths mashed against each other's, tongues thrashing around with pure passion. It was me. I had to believe that I was worth something. Maybe it was destiny. Maybe God had finally answered my prayers and sent Everett into my life before it was too late.

"Home, now," he said.

I obliged and turned to walk away. He stopped me, picked me up, and waved down a taxi. He placed me delicately into the cab, and we headed home to Azul Towers.

When we arrived at our destination, he picked me up once again and headed to the twentieth floor. As we crossed the threshold, he put me down and looked me in the eye.

"I love you. You make my world different. I'm not sure why or how or anything, but the only thing I'm certain about is you.

You're beautiful, intelligent, strong, and worthy of love. You have to believe that before I can give it to you," he said.

"I love you too," I said.

He grabbed my cheeks, welcoming me again for another kiss. The emotional pain from earlier had subsided, and I was sure of one thing in my life. Everett Patrick Brown.

He unzipped my cocktail dress and let it pool to the floor. I stepped out of my black pumps, and he bent down and licked the blood on the scrape that was on my right knee. His hands made their way up my thighs then to my black thong panties. He moved it aside and draped my right leg over his shoulder, making love to me with his perfect mouth. My loud sounds of pleasure echoed throughout the foyer of his place. I felt the impending feeling of ecstasy building up in my core. My body went limp, and I came, hard in his mouth. He sucked up every last drop and stood.

He yanked my panties off, dropped his suit pants, and pinned me to the wall.

"I fucking love you, Lyla."

"Ahhhh, fuck!" I screamed as he thrust himself into me. "I love you, Everett," I cried as I came again, drenching him with my arousal.

He continued pumping into me harder and harder against the wall and let himself go into my welcoming body.

I was sure at that moment that we were meant for each other. It had to be fate. I needed to understand that there wasn't always an answer for everything. I had to love myself before I allowed him to love me. I was on my way to doing so. I wanted nothing more than his love. He was curing me.

So what if he wanted out of his structured life? I didn't care. I knew he loved me. And I knew I loved him more than all the stars in the universe.

Chapter 8

WORK SEEMED TO drag on the next few weeks. I couldn't wait to get off of work to meet the man I had just fallen in love with. The man whose eyes met mine weeks before and changed me forever. It seemed as if I were waiting every day for something bad to happen. I was used to fucking shit up in my life, and I was sure that I would mess the only positive thing in my life.

He was everything I never recognized and I always desired.

ON A GLOOMY and rainy Monday morning, I arrived at the office fifteen minutes early and prepared Mr. Thomas's coffee as he liked. I had developed a good routine the past two months as his personal assistant, and so far things were mellow. That's how I wanted them to stay.

He came strolling in about thirty minutes after my arrival and placed his body in his thousand-dollar chair behind his massive desk. I positioned his beverage on the table, trying not to make eye contact. He gave me the creeps, but I had to get through the next few months, hoping that I would get a better offer at another firm. I just had to get some experience under my belt.

I was wearing a navy skirt, shorter than the one I wore on my first day, which I knew would delight him. I wore a cream-colored shirt with matching navy business suit jacket and my cream-colored Jimmy Choos, which I had bought the week before. They cost more than what I made in a week. I topped it off with my large, diamond hoop earrings that my mom got me for Christmas the year before.

The day proved to be as uneventful as the others, which was good. I completed all my job duties with fervor and organization. I was ready to get Monday over with so I could meet my boyfriend at a new Mediterranean restaurant for dinner and a few cocktails. We had been together for two months, and they were the happiest two months of my existence.

All had gone smoothly that Monday, and five o'clock was nearing. I suddenly had a terrible feeling in the pit of my gut. The next thing I knew, everyone else was gone from the office, and it was just me and *him*. I wanted to grab my purse and hit the ground running, but my body was frozen. I couldn't move.

He whistled at me, motioning me into his office.

"Yes, Mr. Thomas?" I asked, entering his office.

He pulled out a remote and pointed it toward the corner in his office. He pushed a few buttons and then walked over to stand behind me, remaining completely silent.

I could feel him breathing down my neck, and his breath smelled strongly of alcohol. He had more than likely been sipping on too much of that amber-colored liquor all day.

He touched my neck with his large hands, moving slowly down my spine and back, and ending up at the bottom of my skirt. I was stuck like a statue, terrified of what was going to happen next. What this really happening to me *again*? Was I doing something wrong to attract these dirt bags?

The next thirty minutes were a blur. I blocked the encounter out mentally, or tried my best to. I was supposed to meet Everett for dinner, but I couldn't even call him to cancel it. I sent him a text apologizing and said I was feeling under the weather.

Next thing I knew, I was in my bathtub, crying my eyes out. I made my way out of the tub dripping wet and into my tiny kitchen, still naked. I grabbed a steak knife, placed it on my imperfect and scarred stomach, and cut. After the blood started seeping out of the self-induced wound, I made my way into my bedroom and passed out.

"STEP OUT WITH your hands up, Miss Harper," said Sgt. Davis Moore.

He was the son of the former police chief where I grew up. I did as I was instructed. He pulled me over on a desolate back road. I had been drinking and snorting cocaine. I got out of my car.

"Spread your legs and put your hands on the hood of your car, Lyla," he said.

I did as he asked. I was halfway buzzed, so I didn't realize the rough feeling in the air. That didn't come until seconds later; after all, my reflexes were sluggish from the poison I had just snorted up my nose.

"Do you want another minor consumption, Miss Harper? Perhaps drug possession? That will be far worse for you than a drinking ticket. I am quite sure that you will disappoint your parents very much. Who knows, maybe it will affect your grades, and your grades are definitely a reflection on scholarships. You wouldn't want to screw up senior year, would you?" I said nothing. I lost my breath, and I was panicking.

What a nice birthday present for me. I was losing my innocence on my eighteenth birthday.

He proceeded to grab my breasts. I cringed and tried to push him away, but he was too strong. I strained to get the words out of my mouth to scream, to tell him no, but I couldn't. Besides, we were in the middle of a fucking back road. Who would hear me? There was nothing but corn fields and old coal mines around. He threw me to the ground, tore my jeans off, and pinned himself on top of me. That was the beginning of my *problem*.

I WOKE UP screaming. I hadn't had a flashback in some time. I didn't know what to do, but in a quick knee-jerk reaction, I picked up my cell phone and dialed Everett. I wanted him to save me from myself.

Chapter 9

"LYLA, ARE YOU feeling better? Want me to bring you something to eat?"

I didn't respond, I only cried.

"I'm on my way." He cared. He was going to shield me from myself and help me through my past.

Within ten minutes, there was a knock at my door. I pulled on my robe and tried to wipe off the black mascara that had run down my puffy, reddened face. My eyes were swollen from crying, but I didn't care what I looked like. I just wanted him. I opened the door with tears still strolling down my cheeks, and he hugged me. It was then that I knew everything was going to be all right because I had him.

"What's going on, Lyla? Are you hurt? Please tell me," he urged.

"No, I'm not okay, but I will be because I have you," I said, throwing myself into his arms.

I decided not to tell him about Mr. Thomas. At least not yet. I had to start from the beginning, the very beginning. I had to tell him about my father and my *problem*.

"I think you've realized that I've avoided certain questions the past two months. Questions centering on my father and his death. Others about my hometown and why I haven't visited in four years. I think now is the time I confront those things and tell you.

"Like I said, I love my family. They're so important to me. I've given them so much grief since I was seventeen. I got a minor consumption junior year when I was seventeen, and the next year things just got worse. A lot was my fault. I blamed my father's suicide for my behavior in high school. I was a good student but got into some drinking and drugs.

"I had, well still have, some major body image issues, and it got worse the summer before senior year. I was drinking and snorting cocaine by myself on one of my favorite back roads on my eighteenth birthday. I saw the police lights in my rearview mirror. I wasn't too worried about it until Davis Moore, a cop and the former police chief's son, was the officer. His dad and Rick are great friends.

"A lot of girls swooned over him, but I wasn't one of them at all. He was young, only twenty-two at the time. Still not an excuse for what happened."

Everett continued to eye me as I was talking, clearly following me and listening to my story intently.

"He asked me about my former minor consumption. He knew I had been drinking and doing drugs and threatened to tell my parents and have my scholarships taken away. I couldn't allow him to do that to me. They were the only way for me to get out of Rigdon and start a new life.

"He told me to step out of the car, and when I did … I uh, he grabbed my breasts, pinned me down, and took my virginity on my eighteenth birthday. That was the start of the coercion. It continued through senior year. As soon as I graduated from high school, I moved to Chicago and spent the summer before classes started working at a local coffee shop."

"Lyla, I am so sorry. You deserve to be treated like a princess. I cannot imagine why someone would want to do something so horrendous. You are the strongest person I know. How you have overcame all this is beyond me. You astound me, Lyla Elizabeth."

He hugged me, and I saw that there was a glimmer of a tear in his emerald eyes. I embraced his hug but had to finish what I started.

"I need to tell you why I resorted to self-mutilation and drinking. I have severe body image issues, and when everything started with Davis, it just got worse. I had no self-esteem. I didn't feel like I was worthy for anyone. Cutting myself seemed to take away the pain … at least for a brief amount of time.

"Sometimes I feel like if I hadn't started all that shit, Davis wouldn't have done what he had done. Shit, Rosalynn overcame everything, went to college, became a nurse, and got married. She has the whole perfect family, husband, and house with a fucking white picket fence. I wonder every day why I wasn't strong enough to swallow it all and take it as a grain of salt. Garrett was pretty good too until he went to Iraq and lost his best friend. He hasn't been the same since then.

"It happened when I was six. My father was brilliant, making a lot of money, but we never saw any of it. He was an industrial engineer and worked seventy-plus hours a week. He drank too much and cared too little.

"He was very hard on us all, especially my mother. He terrified us, made us all feel unworthy. We were living in Nebraska at the time because my father's job took us there. All my cousins and grandparents remained in Kansas. He would beat the living shit out of my mom, day after day. Then he started in on us. I remember one time when I was little, my father was working on something in the garage. I wanted to help him, but I guess I was just a bother. He didn't want to deal with me. He got up screaming at me and threw the hammer at me. The back end of it sliced my calf. I ended up with twenty stitches. That's when Mom had enough. She was ready to leave.

"It was a cold December night, just one week before Christmas. Mom had it all planned out, to leave just before he got home from work. Plans changed when Dad came home early, drunk and pissed off. He saw our bags and knew Mom's plans. He went into his bedroom and grabbed his .22 shotgun, loaded it, and shot at my mother. Thankfully he missed. We ran into the bathroom and locked the door, praying that it would end. We heard another shot and then sheer silence for what seemed like forever. My mother walked out of the bathroom, and I heard her scream. She tried to keep us in the bathroom, but I pushed my way out. I saw my father lying there, dead. He shot himself in the chest. There was blood everywhere. My dad had killed himself in a drunken rage, but tried to kill my mom first."

I was very matter of fact about it all. I was more apprehensive about Everett's response than the trauma I had encountered as a young child. I was waiting for him to say something, anything. He looked at me with such disbelief.

"So are you ready to leave yet?" I asked with sadness in my voice.

"Absolutely not, Lyla. I want to know everything about you, the good and the bad. Besides, you can't help what happened to you; you were just a child. You didn't ask to be brought into this world by your parents; they brought you into it. None of that is your fault. Words cannot describe how sorry I am for the circumstances that surrounded your childhood, but I have to say I am so glad that your parents did bring you into this world. You are my world now. Come here," he said with remorse in his voice.

I did as I was told. It felt good to listen to someone who cared for me. He held me in his loving arms, and I drifted off to sleep.

I awoke sweating with anxiety. I looked over to my right and saw my sweet Everett sleeping like an angel. I felt at ease in his company. He started stirring in his sleep.

"What are you doing up?" he asked, rubbing his dark lashes.

"Couldn't sleep, too much on my mind," I responded with distance.

"Lyla, is something else on your mind? Want to talk about it?"

"I'm not nearly ready, Everett. I'm too scared of losing you. I'm terrified at the thought of you leaving me once you know everything about me. I'm broken, too far gone … that's how I felt until I met you. I know this is probably too much for you to hear considering the amount of time we've known each other, but …"

"No buts, Lyla. I feel the same way about you. My past isn't all peachy either. Everyone has demons in their past."

He hugged me and brushed my hair out of my face. He bent down to kiss me. I wanted him so badly but felt like a dirty whore after what happened the previous day. It was my fault, that's how I felt. If I had done what Mr. Asshole Pervert asked, he probably wouldn't have had his way with me. I wasn't returning to my internship, no questions asked. I had to find a way to figure it out, and I would. As long as I had Everett, anything was possible.

I turned away when he tried to kiss me, and he looked perplexed. I had to find a way to explain to him what happened to me, but I was afraid. I was terrified of losing him because of the darkness of my past and the darkness within me.

"Lyla?" He looked heartbroken.

"I'm so sorry, Everett. There's more that you need to know about me, but I have already told so much more than I ever thought I could share with someone. No one knows any of this about me, except you. I'm not able to do much more. I don't think I'm strong enough to tell you."

"You *are* strong. You will continue to be strong because that's who you are. It's just going to be easier now because you don't have to be alone anymore. You have me. I want to make you happy. If I could make you forget all the bad things that happened to you, I would. I want to make you the happiest woman ever. You make me want to be a better man."

I gave him a swift kiss on the lips, making sure it didn't end up into something more. I had to tell him about what happened with my boss.

"I was doing a lot better, as far as coping is concerned until … well, until yesterday," I said with disappointment in my voice.

"What happened, Lyla? Did someone hurt you?" he said.

"I was sexually coerced by my boss at the ad agency," I replied. There was dead silence.

I didn't know what to do. This gorgeous man was sitting before me, someone whom I knew less than three months, and he suddenly knew my life story. He knew things about me that no one else did. I shared my deepest, darkest secrets with this god of a man, and he looked at me like he wanted to protect me from everyone, including myself.

"Jesus, Lyla! What do you mean by coercion? Were you raped? God damn, you have to go to the police!" he exclaimed with sudden anger in his voice.

"You don't understand. I can't just go to the police. They won't believe me. Besides, he's a millionaire, and I'm positive that's in his favor. Who are they going to side with? An intern who cried rape after a few months on the job or a wealthy public relations and marketing mogul with money? Come on, Everett. I've dealt with this before. It's all about who knows who, and I don't know anyone."

"Lyla, you have to tell someone!"

"I did. I just told you," I said shakily.

"You can't let him get away with it! Who is it? Tell me now!" he demanded.

I'd never seen that look in his eyes before. They were bright green with fury. For a moment I was scared, and I knew he saw it on my face.

"I'm so sorry, Lyla. I didn't mean to frighten you. I just want to protect you. I want to get that creep."

I wasn't ready to give out names. I had done enough. I couldn't summon the words off my tongue. That pervert did not deserve for his name to be spoken on my lips.

"I'm not going back there," I said grimly.

"Of course you aren't!" he exclaimed.

"I have to figure out a job, apply for some new internship, I guess," I said. "I could always go back to the coffee shop I used to work at. The people there were nice."

"We'll figure this out, Lyla. You aren't alone. When are you going to realize that?" he urged.

"I'm not used to talking about feelings. It's hard for me to accept that someone can take me for everything. Why do you want me anyway? I'm no good for you. You could probably have any woman you wanted. Why would you need me? Full-figured, hardly rail thin, scarred physically and mentally … Why?"

"I cannot stay away from you. Don't say those things about yourself. You're ideal in every way possible. I've never felt this way before. You're beautiful. I knew the moment I saw your gorgeous brown eyes. I felt it as soon as I saw you. When are you going to see that?" he said.

I said nothing. Our eyes met again, and I was drawn to him. He was mine, in my bed, sharing my secrets, telling me I was worth something. I was glad God brought him to me. I was finally trusting a man. I felt like I had known him forever. I was in love with Everett Brown.

Chapter 10

HE HELD ME all night, rubbing my back, giving me encouragement. For once in my life, I felt safe. Safe with him. I was getting hooked on him, his touch, his love, his look, and his everything. He was consuming me, and I never wanted it to end.

He called in sick the next morning for personal reasons. I urged him not to but was secretly glad that he did. We could spend yet another day together. I was sure I would never tire of him. His lovely eyes, amazing body, oh-so-perfect dark hair, and the way he moved when he made love to me. I was in heaven.

"Hey," he said, yawning with a smirk.

"Wow, glad you're still here," I replied with sarcasm in my voice.

I was sure that I would wake up alone in an empty bed without Everett. But he proved me wrong.

"I don't think I could ever get enough of you, Lyla," he said while caressing my arm.

He then proceeded to remove my tank top. I wasn't wearing a bra. It felt awkward, him gawking at me like that. But I soon felt liberated, wonderful, and remarkable even. I was his, and he was mine.

"Come here," he said with obvious want in his voice.

I stood up, our chests skin to skin. He kissed me so gently, yet with so much passion and love. He removed my sweatpants, touching me, wanting me more. My body responded, and I groaned. I pushed him down onto the bed and kissed his lips, neck, and rock-hard stomach. He clearly worked out, and gosh his skin tasted sweet. He was perfection.

"Are you sure? I don't think we should do this," he said.

"Yes, please. Nothing besides you can make it go away. I need you," I urged.

Nothing would help me get over what happened days before like his lovemaking. It was healing both physically and emotionally. I was glad at that point that he hadn't tried anything anal.

We made love to each other over and over all day long. His touch masked the hurt and abuse I had felt days before. Our bodies spooned and cuddled. It felt true. I was happy and safe in his arms. I was in love.

"What am I to do with you, Lyla Harper?" he said happily.

"Ha, is that an invitation, Mr. Brown?"

"Always," he replied with a grin.

He kissed me on my forehead. Looking at me, into my soul. It was divine. His eyes meeting mine.

"I sort of promised my mom I would come to her place tonight for dinner. It's usually the type of thing I avoid, but she begged me to. I haven't seen her in over a month, so I conceded. Will you accompany me? I totally understand if you're not feeling up to it. I can call her to reschedule. I'd rather be where you're most comfortable."

I couldn't believe he was asking me to meet his mother! I wanted to spend every waking moment with him, the man who saved me.

"Sure, yeah … I'll go. What time?" I figured getting out of the apartment would do me some good. I needed to avoid being a recluse and re-enter human civilization. I could cope as long as I had my lover at my side.

"Seven, and until then, you are mine, Miss Harper," he said with passion.

He made me feel so good, physically, mentally, emotionally, in every way humanly possible. He took me to the couch and laid me on my back, touching every inch of me. I wanted to scream in ecstasy every time his fingertip affected me. His perfect lips made their way down to the most intimate part of my body, and he kissed me with purity. I screamed out in words that probably made no sense, but I didn't have a care in the world. My Everett was making love to me with his mouth, and I was in heaven.

We got into the shower together. I was feeling nervous, deciding in my head what I should wear. I didn't think I could wear a skirt again and still feel the same about myself after Thomas's demands and eventual coercion.

"Don't be nervous, baby. I know she'll adore you, just as I do." He smiled. It was as if he could sense my nervousness.

"I know. I'm just deciding what to wear," I replied while rinsing the shampoo out of my long, black hair.

"You would look lovely in anything you choose," he said, hugging my naked, wet body.

We got out of the shower, and he wrapped a towel around his hips and then lay on the bed, watching my every move and grinning the whole time. I wrapped my pink fluffy robe around my body and made my way over to my closet. I thought for a few minutes about what to wear.

I went with a knee-length black cocktail dress and black pumps. Formal and sexy. I wanted to look good for him. I dressed and straightened my hair and applied my smoky eye makeup and red lipstick.

"You choose red lipstick, Lyla? Now I cannot kiss you until later," he said, smiling sweetly at me, still wrapped in his towel.

"You need to get dressed, Everett. Want to head upstairs to your place?"

"Sure, let's go," he said, unwrapping his towel and putting on his jeans … no underwear again! Ahh! I wanted to take him to my bed once more, but I knew that would happen later. He put on his T-shirt and took my hand. We headed upstairs to the twentieth floor. I started to get butterflies in my stomach. I loved his apartment so much more than mine. It was so much nicer.

We headed to the twentieth floor, apartment 4024. We walked into his place. It was considerably lovelier than mine. He noticeably had more money than I did. His apartment was clean and modern. His furniture looked brand-new, and he had a full-wall bookshelf jam-packed with books, dictionaries, thesauruses, and law books. Next to the shelf, there were several guitars on stands.

"Play for me," I said sweetly.

"Now?" he asked.

I nodded. He grabbed an acoustic guitar off one of the stands. He started strumming the strings with his powerful fingers. *Wow, I know what I could do with those,* I thought, giggling to myself.

"This song is for you, baby," he said. *"Slipped on my shoes and I made myself look somewhat right, 'cause I can't be at home tonight … and I have no clue as to what I'm doin' here, let me lay on your bed for a day, 'cause it's a long time still until tomorrow. All my insecurities are breaking me up inside. You light another cigarette, and my eyes are on fire. Lightning strikes me only in waves, and I know that I'm safe for now, but I know the rest is on its way. I know it isn't easy, nothing is the way I want it. All this will pass 'cause it's only as the day is long,"* he sang.

Oh my gosh. He was playing "Only as the Day Is Long" by Sera Cahoone. *I love that song. This man is amazing! And he is serenading me with these sweet words*. I was melting in all the wrong places. I wanted him in every way imaginable.

After singing to me, he placed the guitar back on the stand and made his way through the kitchen down the hall, taking my hand in his. I was smiling from ear to ear.

The stainless steel appliances were clearly brand-new and expensive. To the right of the kitchen was a glass dining table that sat six. Down the hall was his bedroom. In the middle stood a large four-post bed with a crisp white linen duvet. I was fantasizing about wanting to jump into bed with him right then and there and make passionate love to him like I had done hours before, but I knew that meeting his mother was important. Damn!

Off his bedroom was a large master bathroom with a claw-foot tub and a stand-up shower made of marble. Wow. I was imagining myself in the tub with him, his arms around mine, soaking, relaxing, loving each other.

He was fishing in his large walk-in closet, trying to find something to wear. He donned black suit pants, a light blue button-up dress shirt, and a black tie. He put on his Kenneth Cole dress shoes and topped it off with a sparkling Rolex watch. I was admiring him. He had been mine and still was. I loved him.

"Ready?" he asked, interrupting my daydream.

"Yep!" I said happily, forgetting about what had happened to me days and years before.

He was taking the hurt away from me, and I was finally learning to love myself. I had never thought it was possible.

We got into his black Mercedes S600. Sleek and sexy, just like him. Gosh, I was sure he would cringe in my 1997 Toyota Corolla. We headed north out of the city toward a suburb near the Gold Coast. We held hands the entire way. I could feel my cheeks tire, as I had never smiled as much as I did in the past several hours. We arrived in an area with beautiful mansion homes with perfectly manicured lawns and gates guarding their castles.

I was way out of my league. I thought my stepfather had money, but that wasn't anything compared to city money. Growing up in a tiny Midwestern town with money wasn't the same as how Everett grew up. BMWs, prep schools, and vacationing in Europe were the norm.

We pulled into a long gated driveway. He punched in a code, and the iron security gates opened. We drove up the drive with magnolia trees lining both sides. He circled around the drive, parking his car. He got out and opened my door.

"Miss Harper," he said with his arm out.

I smiled at him and looped my arm around his. We went to the front door, and he opened it. His mother walked toward us, glowing. She was beautiful, tall, and lean, with short, bobbed dark hair and his green eyes.

"Hello. I'm Marie, Everett's mother."

"Lyla Harper," I replied with a smile.

"So very nice to meet you, darling. I am delighted that you came with Everett to accompany us to dinner."

We sat in the living area, and Everett brought me a glass of champagne. My nerves started to dwindle and then I heard a familiar voice. My gut started churning, and I had the sudden urge to vomit. I wasn't sure what was happening to me, but I felt the giddiness and happiness fade quickly.

"Lyla, dear. Come, meet my husband, Michael," she said cheerfully.

It was him. Mr. Asshole Pervert, my old boss. Mr. Thomas, the guy who raped me. I had fallen in love with his stepson.

Chapter 11

MR. THOMAS LOOKED at me with surprise and disgust. I was frozen and didn't know what to do. He held his hand toward mine, expecting me to shake it.

"Nice to meet you, Miss Harper," he said with threat in his tone.

I was terrified. I was unsure. I was everything that I felt days before. I thought those feelings were gone, but they resurfaced because I was at his house, with his stepson who had swept me off my feet. Everett had made me feel whole again.

I didn't extend my hand to his, instead staring straight ahead.

"Lyla?" Everett said.

"Excuse me. I'm feeling a bit unwell. Where is the ladies' room?" I asked, trying to cover up the utter shock.

"I'll show you," Mr. Thomas replied.

I didn't know what to do, so I followed him. I tried with every cell in my body to keep my legs from falling to the floor. I was trembling but trying to hide it.

He took me around the corner to the back of the house. I was certain that considering the enormous size of the house there had to be a restroom closer, but I continued to follow him. *Finally a bathroom. Surely he won't touch me here, in his house, when I am here with his stepson.*

"Fancy seeing you here, Lyla. I suppose you don't plan on telling anyone about our little encounter the other evening, do you? After all, who is going to believe a whore like you with a record? I know everything about you."

I didn't respond. Instead, I shook my head, agreeing with him. *Record?* I thought. I had one minor consumption when I was seventeen. How was he able to see that? It wasn't public record because I was underage. *What does this sicko know about me and how?*

I entered the huge, luxurious bathroom and glanced at myself in the mirror, determined not to cry. *Breathe, Lyla! Get through this for Everett.* My knees remained weak, and my face grew pale. I felt the sweat pool over my brow, and my heart was fluttering like crazy. A few more moments and I would be composed enough to leave the restroom and face the demon that turned my world upside down, again.

After being sure that I was okay enough to face Everett, his mother, and Mr. Rapist, I opened the door with Everett gazing at me with obvious worry in his face.

"You okay?" he asked, genuinely concerned.

"Um, yeah, just a headache," I said, dismissing him.

"Ready to eat?" he asked.

"Sure," I said, trying to sound confident.

We spent the next hour eating veal, some sort of parsnip and potato side, and other courses that I didn't care for. I poked at my food, trying to look interested and engaging in conversation when appropriate, but my heart was broken. I knew that there was no way in hell I could have a future with a man whose stepfather was my boss who raped me. That would never work.

The more I thought about it, the more I wanted to cry. But the last thing I wanted to do was to make a scene. I didn't want to hurt Everett, but I knew I had to. I had to end it after dinner, and I wasn't sure what I was going to tell him.

"Nice to meet you, Lyla. I hope to see you again soon," Marie said, kissing me on both cheeks.

"Thank you," I replied, trying to smile.

"Everett, sweetheart, I do miss you. Please come around more."

"Okay, Mom, I'll try. Work has been hectic," he said.

"Goodnight, Everett. Lyla," Michael said sternly, not taking his eyes off me.

We got into Everett's Mercedes S600. I was silent, not sure what to say or do.

"You okay, baby?" he asked.

I didn't reply. Instead, I let out a sob. I wasn't able to control it. All my sorrows, my whole life. I was tired of it. I couldn't ever catch a break. The one good thing that had happened to me had to be taken away. I was so broken that I physically hurt.

"Pull over, Everett. I'm about to be sick."

"What? Lyla, what's going on? Why are you crying?"

"Pull over!"

He pulled over, and I ran out of the car, puking my guts out on the side of the road. My nerves were shot. All I wanted to do was go home, drink a bottle of wine, fall asleep, and never wake up. Life had been too cruel, and I was sure I couldn't handle it much longer. After throwing up, I didn't feel much better. I got back in the car.

"Take me home please," I cried.

"Was it the food?" Everett asked.

"No! Take me home. I warned you. I am messed up. This definitely isn't going to work, Everett. I cannot do this. No more questions. Take me home now."

He said nothing. The drive was silent and seemed like forever with his hands clenched so hard onto the steering wheel that his knuckles were snow white. Finally I saw the city lights and felt a small amount of relief knowing that I was almost home. We got to the building, and I got out of the car, not saying anything, not turning back. I knew I couldn't face him with those piercing green eyes.

I ran inside, went up to my apartment, stripped off my clothes, and hopped into a hot bath. I felt dirty again, seeing Michael Thomas, feeling guilt-ridden like it had all been my doing. My hands ran down to my stomach, and I cowered, feeling the scars. I needed to do it again, to hurt myself for being such a bad girl, for ruining another good thing in my life. I paused, thinking how everyone would go on without me, how the world would be a better place without Lyla Harper.

I got out of the bath with my body hurting from emotional pain. I went into the kitchen and pulled out a steak knife, pushing it to my imperfect stomach, and cut. No tears this time, no pain, just a release. The feeling of the warm blood dripping down my stomach made me feel better and worse at the same time. I knew I was regressing, but I didn't care. I wasn't sure that I cared about anything anymore.

I popped open a bottle of wine and poured a glass and thought long and hard. Trying to decipher the past week of my life. I had dealt with the *problem* by running away from that shithole town I grew up in and not returning for the past four years. I had always come up with excuses about school or work, good reasons that people believed, in order not to come home around holidays. I couldn't tolerate running into Davis Moore again. I thought I solved that problem by moving away.

But, no. It had to happen again. *Why me?* I thought. *It must be me. Life is not fair.* Why was God punishing me? I turned on my iPod and played Florence and the Machine's "Leave My Body," listening to every word. The lyrics were sung for me at that moment in my life. I thought I was saved, but I was so wrong. I drank the rest of the bottle of Yellow Tail shiraz, stumbled onto my bed, and passed out.

"Mr. Thomas, please don't do this. I can't—"

"Lyla, I had a set of rules. If you would have followed them, then none of this would have happened. This isn't my fault, you know. It's yours. You fucking whore, walking around with your big tits and sweet ass. You were just asking for this," he said with a sick tone.

He grabbed my wrists and twisted me around, immobilizing me in front of his huge desk. My stomach was pushed so hard against the mahogany wood, I felt like I was going to vomit. My lungs felt like they were about to explode. I was trying to focus on breathing in between my loud cries. I wanted to die.

He yanked my skirt up and ripped my panties off. I was sobbing, and the harder I wept, the more he laughed. It was even more disgusting than my encounter with Davis Moore. Hard to believe considering this was the second time I was being raped. At least Davis never beat the shit out of me before taking me.

He slapped my ass repeatedly, making me cry out harder. I heard him tear open a condom packet, and within a few seconds, he slammed his dick into my tight ass. An overwhelming sense of pain shot through my entire body. I quivered from the amount of pain that was shooting through my body.

I was helpless like a bird without wings. I was unable to fly away from this sick bastard.

My body went limp, and I had no choice but to take it. I was pinned, and he was much stronger than me. I felt the trickle of blood from my ass and an unbearable tearing sensation. *I wish God would take me … give me a heart attack and take me out of my misery.*

"Can't get you pregnant like that, you fucking cunt," he said.

I didn't respond with words, but rather with tears in a continuous stream down my swollen, saddened, and broken face. My soul was broken again, possibly forever now.

When he was finished with me, I was slumped over his large mahogany desk, feeling like a dirty whore. He did make me feel like it was my mistake. Why was it so tough for me to follow rules? I had spent most of my life breaking them, and then I go and fuck up again? I lay there for what seemed like an eon, not sure of what to do. He came behind me, pulled my skirt down, and rubbed my back. I wanted to crawl into a hole and never come out.

"You understand not to tell anyone about this, right, Lyla? No one will believe you. Do you know what money can buy? And I have a lot of it. If you tell anyone, I will find you, and I will make you disappear. I know more about you than you think," he said.

"Yes, Mr. Thomas," I replied, shocked and weeping.

My eyes were so swollen from crying that I could barely see. My bottom was raw from his abuse, and my ass was engorged and torn from his force. It hurt to put my legs together and stand up straight. I wanted to get as far away from that dirt bag as I could.

"Go, you fucking skanky-ass slut," he demanded.

I said nothing. I grabbed my purse and did as I was told, hoping that if I listened I wouldn't be punished anymore. I was dazed but made my way to my car, started it, and headed home. I was broken again.

I WOKE UP with a killer hangover. I had gotten used to them though, a champ at self-medicating myself to mask the demons and darkness. I picked up my cell phone. There were six missed calls from Everett and one text message.

Lyla, please let me understand you. I need to know what's going on. I am not going anywhere, and I will not give up on you or on us. I believe in us. Nothing will come between it. I will not allow it. Please call me. I need to hear your voice. I love you more than anything … please.

I sobbed, reading it. Refusing to believe it. Why would he care so much for me? Was it really meant to be? Was Rosalynn right about taking a chance? I wasn't ready to give in yet. How was I supposed to explain to him that his stepfather was the sick bastard that raped me? Would he even believe me? I doubted that he would, even though I knew from what he told me that he didn't care for his stepfather.

Why didn't he tell me what his stepfather did? Why didn't he ask me what firm I worked for? I had so many questions and desperately wanted answers, but I was wounded and in pain. How could anyone understand? *Go figure the one person who knows that I was raped would be Everett, someone I could not end up with.*

I was silly for thinking that he was my prince. After all, I had kissed enough frogs to meet him. Was it really too good to be true? I wanted him, still after everything. But I needed to clear my head first. For the first time in four years, I was going home. I needed my family. I needed to face my past and face Davis Moore.

Chapter 12

"Hey, sweetie!" my mother said with exhilaration in her voice.

"Hey, Mom, I have some news. I'm coming home for a visit," I said.

"What about your new internship, Lyla?"

"There's a lot to explain, Mom. Can I just enlighten you when I get home?" I pleaded.

"Sure, honey, are you okay? You sound troubled."

"I will be, Mom. I always will be," I answered very matter-of-fact.

"Are you going to stay with me and Rick or with Rosalynn and Aidan?"

"I haven't called Rosalynn yet. Figured I would surprise her and the boys," I responded. "Is it all right if I stay with you and Rick?"

"Sure thing, honey. This will always be your home too, you know. No matter what."

I loved my mother. She was the only person in the world that would be able to put a smile on my face after everything I had endured. On several occasions, I had contemplated telling her about Davis Moore, but I felt guilt. I didn't want to make a deal about it. After all, I lived in a small town, and it would never be the same after airing out all the dirty laundry. I didn't want to do that to Rick. He was big in town, contributed a lot to the community. I didn't want to embarrass him.

I packed my bags and popped open another bottle of wine. Nothing like taking care of a hangover with more alcohol. I looked at my phone, trying to decide if I wanted to call Everett to tell him where I was going. I decided against it. I needed to sort things out first and then deal with him. I had thoughts in the back of my head that if I were to go back to Kansas, I wouldn't return to Chicago, but I was willing to take that chance. I needed my mother and sister more than anything else, even more than I needed Everett. I wasn't sure about anything anymore.

Two hours, a bottle of wine, and a pack of Parliaments later, I was all packed. I wanted to leave right then but decided that I had had one too many glasses of wine and that I would leave first thing in the morning. I didn't want to make more trouble for myself with a DUI, so I slumped onto my cozy couch and listened to music, thinking about my life. My mind began to wander.

I started to pray to God. I grew up Catholic. I was strong in my faith even though I had failed to go to church for so many years. My church helped my family and me get through tough times, like after my dad's suicide. My parish raised money to help my mom pay for funeral expenses and a U-Haul to help us move from Nebraska to Kansas.

I needed all the praying in the world. Maybe God would help me understand my life, why it had been so unfair. I remembered my mom always telling me that God never gave us more than we could handle. Could I be that strong to go through everything I had? I didn't want the darkness to win, so I indulged and felt the need to pick up my phone.

My phone started buzzing. I answered with a sorrowful, "Hello?"

"Lyla! What the fuck, girl. I have not heard from you in days. I have tried calling and texting you several times. Are you okay?" asked Anya Ross, my dear friend.

"No, I'm not okay. Dealing with some personal stuff right now," I responded distantly.

"What has happened to you, Lyla? Tell me," she demanded.

"I can't right now, Anya. It would take hours. I'm going home tomorrow to see my family. I promise when I get back that I'll talk with you. I'll tell you everything."

"What the hell, Lyla. I'm trying to be a friend to you right now, but you won't let me. It isn't fair. But I have one more question to ask you," she said.

Butterflies and anxiety started to bubble in my gut.

"I got the weirdest phone call yesterday. He said his name was Michael Thomas and he was your boss at the firm. He was wondering why you have not returned to work the past several days. I told him I didn't know. Then if things could become any more bizarre, he asked if I wanted your job within the firm, to be his personal assistant."

"Fuck, fuck, fuck! Anya, promise me one thing—do not go anywhere near him. Promise me," I cried.

"Calm it, sister. I told him I already have a job and wasn't interested in the least. I was just wondering how he got my number. Kinda weird."

"Promise me, Anya. Never answer his call again and stay as far away from him as possible. When I get home, I promise to tell you everything. I should be home sometime next week," I assured her.

"Okay, Lyla, but you will give me answers. I care about you. You're a great friend. Whatever it is that happened, I want to be there for you."

"Promise," I replied.

The conversation was done, and I prayed that Michael Thomas would stay away from her. She had a good heart and did not deserve to be tainted like I was. She wouldn't be able to handle it. I placed the conversation in the back of my head and focused on facing Everett.

I called Everett, and he answered on the first ring.

"Jesus, Lyla, what the hell is going on?"

I didn't respond. I felt like a total coward and idiot. I hung up the phone. He called me right back, and I answered, not saying anything.

"Lyla, I'm coming down to talk to you right now. If you don't answer the door, I'll wait outside until you do. I need to know that you're okay. I need to know what's going on. I need you," he pleaded.

I didn't respond. I just hung up the phone.

Within three minutes, there was a knock at the door. I froze, not knowing what to do. I walked toward the door and started to unlock it. I took a deep breath, tucked my unruly curly hair behind my ears, wiped my eyes, and opened the door. There he was. Everett, my Everett. Caring for me so much. He looked like a god. His dark hair and heavenly green eyes. I was captivated. I stood there, waiting for him.

He lunged toward me, embracing me, hugging me like it was the last time we would see each other. He took my face into his hands.

"I don't know what's going on, but nothing is going to make me leave you. You need to understand that first. Second, you need to believe and trust in me, in what I say. I care about you like I have never cared about anyone before. So, if you want to talk, we can. If you want to tell me what's bothering you, you can. But if you aren't ready to talk, that's fine too. I'm here for you and will wait for you," he said.

I cried again. Jesus, why was this hot and heavenly man so attentive to me and my needs? I had never met anyone like him before. As I sat there in thought before this gorgeous man, it clicked. Maybe God was answering my prayers. Maybe he brought Everett into my life. I embraced him back, kissing him fervently.

He twirled my hair in his long, perfect fingers, making me tingle. He picked me up, and I wrapped my legs around him, our lips never leaving each other's. He sat on the couch, with me on top of him. He undid my robe, leaving my whole body bare. He looked at me, taking a deep breath, and placed his oh-so-perfect hands on my shoulders, gently massaging me. His hands moved to my breasts and then onto my flawed, scarred, and freshly scabbed stomach.

"Lovely," he said avidly.

My eyes started to well up, but I didn't want to destroy this moment. It seemed impeccable. Suddenly everything started to make sense. I had finally accepted that he was going to be my saving grace and that God had finally responded to my prayers.

His hands then traveled to my thighs. I undid his zipper, exposing him. He pulled me on top of him. I started the wonderful rhythm of up and down, back and forth, feeling his manhood stretching me to my limit, and it was pure, amazing, and beautiful; it was us.

The familiar buildup started in my core, and I released myself around him. He followed suit seconds later. Our eyes were locked, and we knew we loved each other with our entire bodies and souls. I cradled my head in the nook of his neck, breathing in the scent of him and sex.

"What's that?" he asked, pointing to my bags as I still lay on top of him.

"My bags," I replied nonchalantly, getting off of him.

"What for? Are you leaving? Are you leaving me?" he asked cautiously.

"I've got a lot of thinking I need to do. I'm leaving for Kansas in the morning. I need to sort through shit, get my head straight," I replied.

"What the hell, Lyla? You just make love to me but fail to tell me you're leaving me in the morning? I need answers. I need to know what you want," he said sadly.

"I can't explain now, Everett. You won't understand," I said.

"How many fucking times do I have to tell you, I am not going anywhere," he said, slightly irritated.

"It's not as easy as you think. It isn't going to be something you want to hear."

"Try me," he urged.

I lifted myself off of him, putting my robe back on, feeling slightly self-conscious again, like a dirty whore. *No!* I yelled to myself in my head. *Stop! I am not going to destruct this. Just be honest with him, Lyla. If it's meant to be, then it will be. Like Rosalynn said, it's a lessoned learned otherwise.*

I headed toward my fridge and opened it. I grabbed a Heineken, popped the cap, and sauntered back over to him and sat next to him on my couch.

"You might need this," I said, handing him a beer. "This is going to take awhile. First, I just want to apologize for all my baggage. I will approve if you choose not to stay with me after hearing this. It's unfair for me to continue to string you along, sobbing all the time without explanation, so here goes. Your stepfather, how long has he been in advertising?" I asked.

"As long as I've known. What does Michael have to do with any of this?"

Suddenly his skin turned ashen gray and then white. His eyes burned with hatred. He figured it out with my first question. *Shit,* I thought. *He's going to run.*

"Oh my fucking gosh. It was him, wasn't it, Lyla? It makes sense, your behavior at my mother's house the other night. Why in the hell didn't you tell me? Am I that fucking stupid that I didn't figure this out on my own? I'm going to get that fucking bastard. Oh fuck, this is bad, really bad." He stood up and began pacing back and forth.

"Everett, stop!" I cried.

He started to get dressed. He was leaving to confront Michael.

"Stop it!" I pleaded.

"Lyla, your battle is my battle now. I will never let anything like this happen to you ever again, understand? Let me handle this!" he exclaimed.

"Don't leave me, please," I sobbed. "I can't be alone, not now. Please, Everett."

"What the fuck. I cannot believe this shit. I want to fucking kill him, Lyla."

"Everett, you cannot make rash decisions. You have to take your mother into account. This will affect her too. You can't just show up and say, 'Hey, Mom, this girl I started fucking told me your husband raped her.' Don't you understand how that will sound? Preposterous."

"First of all, Lyla, you're not 'some girl I'm fucking.' I'm falling for you … hard. All of you," he said with sincerity.

"Why do I deserve you?" I asked.

"Stop it. When are you going to see what I see? Beauty, grace, intelligence. The list is endless. There's a reason we ended up in the same cab, Lyla—destiny," he said, not taking his eyes off mine.

"What now?" I asked.

"You aren't still going to Kansas, are you?"

"Yes, I need my mother and sister right now. I have got to clear my head … think things through."

"You can't be serious right now. You're going back there knowing that he'll be there? Are you trying to make more trouble for yourself?"

Holy shit, he was pissed. I was pretty sure at that point that we were fighting. What was I supposed to do? Run from my *problem* in Chicago or keep from the *problem* back at home? Confusion was a major understatement for what I was feeling. I had to face it. I had to go home. I needed to tell my mother everything. She was, after all, my biggest supporter despite all my letdowns. I needed her advice, her comfort, and her warmth.

"I need my mother right now. She understands me, Everett. I have to tell her about everything. I need her," I said.

I wanted him to feel that I needed him. I did, but I desired my space. It was a lot to take in. I had fallen in love with the stepson of a multimillion-dollar pervert who raped me. How was that going to work? My subconscious was raging with questions, but I quickly dismissed it. I didn't want my mind to run around in circles. I couldn't modify anything. What happened had happened. I needed to take control of my life for the first time in years. I wasn't going to let Everett go.

"Please understand. I'm not running away from you. I need my mom and sister, my whole family now. I think it's time I told them about Davis. I think they'll understand a lot more if they knew about him. I'm coming home to you, to us," I said with a reassuring tone.

"Lyla, I don't think that's a very good idea. But I'll be the last person to tell you what to do. You're a grown woman. I'm here for you. If you need anything, I'll be there. I'm going to figure this Michael thing out. Just so you know, it's going to take everything I have not to kill that fucking bastard. But he'll get what he deserves, rest assured. Karma is a bitch. I promise nothing is going to happen to you. Nothing will happen to us," he said, grabbing my chin to meet his lips.

There was electricity in the air again. His lips met mine. I couldn't get enough of him; he was my new addiction. The first healthy one I had in a long time. I wanted him forever ... always. My heart stopped every time he touched me, stroked me, fucked me, and kissed me. He was my everything.

"Stay with me tonight before I leave in the morning?" I asked.

"I figured this much," he replied with a grin.

The night went well as we held one another, but I was nauseated and sickened. I managed to throw up a few times. I dismissed it as nerves and climbed back into bed with my lover.

Within an hour or so, I had fallen into a sweet slumber, dreaming of my Everett and our new, honest beginning together.

Chapter 13

EIGHT O'CLOCK CAME too soon. I watched his naked body rise from my bed, admiring what was mine. I didn't want him to go, but I knew what I needed to do. To face my past and finally be honest with my family even though I knew it would hurt them deeply. His perfectly sculpted ass made me feel right in all the wrong places. I got out of bed, naked, all his.

"Come here," I pleaded with blazing eyes.

He walked over to me, obviously happy to do so. I quickly pushed him to the bed, letting him know that I was in control. I pinned his arms above his head, invading his mouth with my all, straddling him at the same time. I was in an utter state of complete high, like no drug I had ever done in my life.

We fucked with carnal rawness, rough and gentle at the same time. He pulled on my hair as he claimed my mouth. I dug my fingernails in his chest, marking him as mine. We came together, Everett shouting my name as I moaned so loudly I was sure New York City could hear me. It was awesome.

"I'm going to miss that," he said.

"You talk as if I'm never coming back," I stated.

"I worry ..."

"I'll be back next week. Promise," I said, holding out my pinky finger.

He clutched it with his. I smiled. He really did make me happy. As much as I didn't want him to go, he did. He had a morning meeting to attend and then court all day.

I grabbed my bags and headed down to my car, determined. I picked up my phone and dialed my mother.

"Hey, Mom!" I said.

"Hey, sweetie! Cannot wait to see you. About eight or so hours?"

"Yep … cannot wait, Mom. There's so much we need to catch up on."

"Drive safely, Lyla!"

"Always, Mom," I said.

I was heading out of the city. Sudden relief took over my body. I was glad to be out of the city limits of my latest *problem* but knew it wouldn't last long, as I would be revisiting my old one.

Eight hours, endless cups of coffee, and a pack of cigs later, I arrived in my hometown of Rigdon, Kansas, population 4,400. Nervousness rested in my stomach, but I was prepared to face the past, ready to start my future and put all the demons behind me. I was ready to be straightforward with my family; maybe that would give them a better understanding of my self-destructive behavior.

I pulled my car into my parents' long driveway. Their home was situated on thirty acres of old coal mining land. It was breathtaking. Large pine trees lined the drive, and the smell of the sweet country air made me smile. A large three-acre lake was nestled below the hills of their home with a tall and full weeping willow tree on the right.

I couldn't believe I hadn't been home in four years. I didn't realize just how much I missed it there. The smell and the slow pace of things. It made me realize how much I didn't appreciate it when I lived there.

"My darling!" my mother exclaimed, waiting for me on the huge wraparound porch.

"Hi, Mom!" I said with tears streaming down my face.

I had missed her so much, it hurt. She was my rock, accepting me through thick and thin. I was her daughter and her friend, which made our relationship stronger. For a moment, I was sad that I didn't share everything with her. I felt as if I failed her, like I was dishonest. I wasn't exactly that, just withheld some truth, a lot of truth. I was ready to tell her.

"How was the drive, Ly?"

"So long. I'm so happy to be home. It's been too long. Where's Rick?"

"At the VFW, eating their monthly catfish supper," she said, slightly annoyed.

I was kind of relieved, knowing I didn't have to look him in the eye. I wasn't ready yet. I was trying to understand how I would tell them. I sure as hell wasn't going to bombard them on the first evening home. I wanted to see my sister and her family as well as my brother. I missed them dearly.

"I'm so excited to surprise Ros and her family. Where's Garrett?" I asked.

Garrett was older than me by two years, and we were less close than Rosalynn and I, but we remained in contact over the years. He had his own battles being a marine, fighting overseas, and losing his best friend in front of him from a roadside bomb. He, no doubt, had a closet full of his own demons, and I sure as hell didn't want to load more of my shit onto him. He was my brother, and I loved him deeply like my sister, just in a different way.

"I have a surprise for you, Lyla!" my mother said.

"What's going on?" I replied.

"Well, I have a little get-together planned at King's tonight. Everyone will be there. They are all so delighted that you came

87

home for a visit. I couldn't keep it from Rosalynn and Garrett. I hope you don't mind."

Gosh damnit, Mom! I thought. The last thing I wanted to do was hang out at the town's only bar. I was surely going to run into some bitches from high school, and I wasn't about to make small talk with them. I recognized she wanted to make me happy, that she too was happy that I came home … but really?

"Um, okay … sounds good. What time?" I said, trying not to sound disappointed.

"Get dressed, sweetie. Then we can be on our way! Everyone is waiting for you!" she exclaimed.

I went upstairs and headed down the long hallway. My old bedroom was the last room on the left. I wondered if it was the same as I left it. I felt a small amount of fear before opening the door. There had been so many memories there, most of them bad. I remembered crying on my bed, drunk, high, and cutting … a lot. I was unsure how I felt about sleeping in there, but I was determined to put it behind me so I could focus on my new future with Mr. Perfect. Just thinking of him made me blush and tingle.

I opened the door and saw that my full-size bed remained in the middle of the room with a dark purple down comforter. There were fresh vacuum marks on the beige carpet. It was obvious that my mother had just cleaned and dusted it. To the right was my old computer desk decorated with photos from high school. One photo was me and my friends from the cheer team making silly faces. That was sophomore year, happier times before the *problem* entered my life.

Above my bed hung a large six foot by five foot, black and white poster of Dave Matthews. To the left next to the picture window was a collage of Marilyn Monroe photographs. I smiled when I saw them; she was my idol.

I laid my suitcase on the bed and unzipped it. I was contemplating what to wear that night. Definitely nothing too sexy. After all, my man was in Chicago, so I didn't have anyone to impress. I pulled out my torn skinny jeans and pink cloth wedges with a black, long-sleeved fitted shirt. I pulled my hair back into a bun, put on my clothes, and put on black hoop earrings and matching pale pink lip gloss. I was as ready as I'd ever be.

"I'm ready, Mom," I said.

"Oh, honey, you look beautiful!"

"Thanks, mom," I said, trying not to blush.

Ten minutes after getting into the car, we arrived at King's Bar. It was situated on the town square on the corner. The building was over a hundred years old. It definitely had character. The outside had a tacky green neon sign that said: "King's Bar, smoking permitted." How hilarious that smoking was still allowed, that they used it as a selling point. Even if it hadn't been permissible, I was sure people would still do it.

Butterflies were swarming my belly as I stepped out of my mother's car. I walked behind her, with obvious self-consciousness, and she opened the front door. It smelled of smoke and stale beer.

"Lyla!" Rosalynn exclaimed. She came running toward me with her arms out.

"Hey, Ros," I said with tears starting to well up in my eyes.

"Hey, Aidan!" He had made his way over next to my sister with his arm around her waist. He was a handsome man, with dirty brown hair in a fresh fade. Very clean cut. He was good for my sister and made her happy. I was glad for that.

"Hey, Lyla, glad you decided to come home for an impromptu visit. It took Ros everything she had not to call and bitch you out for not telling her."

"I was going to surprise everyone," I said, reassuring Rosalynn.

I knew she was slightly disappointed since we didn't keep much from each other. Well, except my *problem*. It was going to be difficult telling her too.

"Garrett!" I shouted.

He was over at one of the two pool tables, deep in thought. He was probably betting the rest of his paycheck on that game. I felt for his soul.

"Lyla! So glad you're here," he said. He was clearly already drunk, but he had an amazing way of hiding it.

"Garrett, it's so good to see you. I've really missed everyone," I said, looking around the bar, secretly trying to eye any old foe or fuck in the bar.

Thankfully there weren't any, but it was early, only eight o'clock, so it was nearly inevitable that someone I didn't want to see was going to show up.

I walked up to the bar trying to make the decision between beer and wine. I went with beer because wine always made me more emotional.

"Kenny, I'll take a Bud Light fish bowl please," I said to the bartender.

Kenny Walker had been the owner and bartender forever. He was a nice man with long white hair that was pulled into a low ponytail. He had a tendency to be inappropriate at times, especially when a girl had too many bottles of beer. His intentions were never ill though. He owned the place along with his wife, Tina. She was a riot.

"Lyla! How many years has it been? I see Garrett in here all the time, always ask him how you are. He always says the same thing—living the life in the Windy City!" he said with a smoker's chuckle.

"Thanks, Kenny," I said, handing him my money.

"This one is on the house, Lyla. You really should come home more."

"Thanks, Kenny, and I'll try." *Yeah right*, I thought.

I was only coming home to face my demons so I could finally put them behind me, forget them, and move on. I wasn't really thinking about the next five minutes; I was just trying to get through each second. And even that seemed like a struggle. I was ready for the beer to kick in.

We sat at a large table, my family and I, catching up. We talked a lot about my sister's boys, Deric and Daniel. They were the apple of my mother's eyes. We all adored them. I was so proud of the woman my sister had become. She was a good mother, wife, sister, daughter—the list was endless. She was a genuinely good person. She was able to put my father's horrific abuse and suicide aside to live her life happily. I was hoping to soon do the same.

I pulled my cell out of my Coach purse. I had seven missed calls, all from Everett. "Shit," I said to myself. I was supposed to call him when I got there safely. I decided to excuse myself for the bathroom and call him. I wasn't ready to explain my relationship with him to my family. They wouldn't understand it. They would just think I was jumping into something too fast again, story of my life.

"Everett?" I said, trying to articulate my words perfectly.

"Lyla, what the hell. I've been worried sick. I suppose you made it to your mother's safely?" he asked.

"Yes, thank you for worrying about me. I'm just catching up with the family. I miss you already. I wish you were here with me," I said.

"Me too, me too, baby. I've got business to attend to here."

I knew he was referring to the Michael fiasco. But I didn't want to go there, not tonight. I had to face what was in front of me, and that was Davis Moore.

"Call me in the morning?" he asked.

"Sure, first thing," I said.

I loved it that he cared about my well-being. I didn't want to know what he was planning for Michael; I just wanted him to first think it through. He did, after all, have his mother to worry about.

I headed back to the table, feeling buzzed and more at ease. I looked up and froze. It was him, my first *problem*, Davis Moore. He was an attractive man, but I couldn't let that justify his actions. I had to confront him. I had to tell my family.

Chapter 14

"LYLA?" HE SAID, puzzled.

"Davis," I replied sternly. "I, um, uh, have to get back to my uh, family," I stuttered.

"Wait," he said, grabbing my arm.

I wanted to reach across and punch him in his face as hard as I possibly could, but that wasn't the way I wanted it to go down. I didn't want to make a scene.

"What, Davis?"

"I uh, I'm glad to see you home," he said with slight remorse in his voice.

"Like I said, I have to get back to my family," I said coldly.

I walked back to the table, trying not to wear my emotions on my sleeve. I sat there, trying to pay attention to what everyone was talking about, but found my eyes wandering over to the corner of the bar where Davis sat with some of his friends. He was only twenty-two, a new and young cop, when the coercion started. *What the fuck*, I thought. *Am I seriously sitting here trying to make excuses for this man who stole my innocence?*

His cop status, bloodline, and good looks were not a justification for what he did to me. I wanted him to know that. I wanted to tell him how I felt. Some more liquid courage, I thought, and that could be a good possibility.

"Excuse me. I have to go to the restroom," I said again.

"Man, Lyla, you really know how to put those beers back," yelled my brother.

I raised my glass as if giving him a cheer. If he only knew how much I really drank. Ha, I could out-drink him any day. I was a pro. It helped me forget about everything, made things more cloudy.

I did my business and washed my hands. I took a long look at myself in the mirror. I criticized my hips, boobs, and ass. It's what I did every time I looked at myself. I knew I was pretty but was so fucked up that I had body image issues ... until I met him, my sweet Everett. He made me feel perfect through all my imperfections.

I applied more pale pink lip gloss and re-did my hair in a messy ponytail, trying to tame my curls that had erupted from my sweating in a tiny, packed bar.

I walked out of the restroom and looked up, annoyed at what I saw. I tried to walk away, but that fucker had to open up his mouth.

"Lyla, wait," said Davis in a husky voice.

"What the fuck do you have to say to me, Davis? Seriously, I doubt that now is the time or the place. But trust me, I have plenty to tell your sorry ass. Fuck off," I said.

My subconscious was proud. I was proud. For the first time, I stood up to him, trying not to notice his muscular build and full pouty lips. *God damn it, Lyla,* I thought again. Was I really looking at that fucker like that? *No,* I thought.

"Lyla, I'm sorry ... it really wasn't like that. You wanted it too; you never said no. If I remember correctly, *you liked it.* I made you come for the first time ..." His voice trailed off.

I couldn't resist it. Before I knew it, my hand met his cheek. I slapped him. Wow, I actually did it. I wanted to jump for joy, but

I knew the entire bar was staring at us. Shit, how the hell was I going to explain this?

I heard a burst of commotion and footsteps make their way to Davis and me. I hardly cared about my outburst to the cocksucker that had scarred me forever, the bastard who stole my virginity and innocence.

"Lyla, what the hell was that? You've had too much to drink!" my mother said, slightly shouting.

"Mom, I'm not going there tonight. Trust me," I said with aggravation.

"Don't use that tone with me."

"Mom, why don't you go ask cop of the year over there what happened to me the summer before senior year on my eighteenth birthday," I yelled, with tears streaming down my face.

I picked up my purse and started to walk out of the bar. I didn't have the time or the energy to try to explain things to Rosalynn or Garrett. I was so glad that Rick wasn't there to see that. It would have been a lot worse. He was good friends with Davis's father. If he knew, blood would really start to boil.

I practically ran out of the bar. Like a knee-jerk reaction, I pulled out my cell and called Everett.

"Hey, baby," he said. God, his voice made me want to fall to my knees.

"Everett, please come to me," I said, sobbing.

"What happened, Lyla?"

"It, um, I uh … I saw Davis at the bar where I was at with my family. He grabbed me. I reacted and slapped him. I kinda got into an argument with my mother, and I left the bar. I'm walking alone now. Please come to me, I need you. I'm so sorry," I said.

"On my way," he replied without hesitation.

IT WAS A Friday afternoon, and I was ready to be out of school. I had an eight ball waiting for me in my car, and it was calling my name. I was ready to snort my coke and mask my misery, at least temporarily. The bell rang, and I practically ran out to my car, ready to get the show on the road. I hit my favorite back road and parked near a school bus turnaround and put my car into park. So much shit had happened in the past few months with Davis that I wanted to forget about it all.

I assembled my cocaine into three perfect lines and carefully rolled a dollar bill, ready to do my business. I swiftly snorted two of the powdered lines before I looked in my rearview mirror and pain settled in my chest. It was *him* again. I knew it was going to happen again, so I quickly snorted the remaining line and waited for him to approach my car. I already had my window down, anticipating our conversation.

"Miss Lyla, I thought you were over this shit. What are we going to do about this?" he questioned me in a flirtatious tone while gesturing toward the powdered residue.

His good looks were obvious, but it made no difference to me. He had already stolen something from me that was impossible to get back. I didn't care how hot he was; he was a sick bastard to me no matter how many women swooned over him.

"Well?" he said.

"I uh, I don't know, Davis ..."

"Come on, baby, step out of the car. You know the drill," he said, opening my door.

I stepped out of my car, and he grabbed my hand, leading me down an old four-wheeler path into the thick woods. He had a blanket tucked under his opposite arm, and I was prepared for what was to come. I had had to endure it several times before.

Thankfully I had time to do a few lines so I would be partially numb. I knew that if I didn't do what he wanted me to, he would stick me with drug possession, and my scholarships would be gone, as well as my ticket out of the hell hole I called home.

We stopped a few minutes after walking to a clearing. He laid the blanket down and stared at me with complete and utter carnal want. My heart went into overdrive, and unease swarmed my belly. I was nervous, scared, vulnerable, and fucked up beyond any comfort. I had to give him what he sought in order for me to get the fuck out of Rigdon, Kansas.

I realized I should just stop with the bullshit alcohol and drugs, but I knew he already had his blackmail, and it wouldn't matter if I was still using or not. He would continue to have his way with me.

"Lay down, gorgeous," he demanded after smoothing the blanket on the dirt.

I did as I was told and lay on top of the blanket, my back feeling the uneven ground beneath me. I stared above, looking at the sky between the many trees, admiring the beauty of the forest, trying to get my mind to focus on something else.

He lay next to me, his hands making their way to the zipper of my jeans. His overbearing, strong fingers unzipped my fly. He bent down to kiss me. I knew better than to resist. I had to give him what he wanted; I had to kiss him back. I tried to fight back the tears but could no longer do it. They began to quietly stream down my face.

He leaned up and looked at me, acknowledging the tears. He said nothing, instead wiped them away with his calloused thumbs. He then proceeded to remove my jeans and panties. His long fingers made their way into my uninvited sex, spreading my folds apart and forcing his fingers inside my tight pussy.

He continued to finger-fuck me, my unwelcome wetness warming his fingers. I desperately tried to keep my legs together, that was my way of saying no, but he was too strong and opened my legs up wider so I was stretched as far as my limber muscles would allow.

My quiet sobs continued.

"Shhh," he said.

I couldn't stop. He didn't care. He was going to have his way with me whether I was crying or silent.

His mouth came apart from mine. My relief was short lived as he trailed unwanted kisses down my scarred and damaged belly, making his way to my sex. He started kissing me in the most intimate part of my body. I was rigid, unwilling to feel it. I was blocking it out the best I could, but the movement of his tongue in and out of my tight opening made my muscles grow rigid, and an unfamiliar buildup started in my core. I released myself, shaking and convulsing uncontrollably while he slipped his tongue out and continued to finger-fuck me.

It was a feeling I had never felt before. I was experiencing my first orgasm by force. My silent sobs grew louder and louder. My lungs felt like they were going to explode. I was sure at that moment that I had died and gone to hell. Why did I let my body respond to him?

Before I had time to compose myself, he forced his dick into my wet sex and came, spurting his fluid into me, letting all his weight down onto my fragile body and battered soul.

"Better go to the clinic tomorrow. I forgot a condom. You need the morning-after pill," he said without any regret.

Chapter 15

B Y THE TIME I arrived at the regional airport outside of town, my feet were throbbing. I didn't care. My sweet Everett was coming to me, to rescue me, to help me. I loved him, and he was falling in love with me. I was sure of it.

After a few hours of waiting, I checked the screen and saw his plane had arrived. I felt like a little girl on Christmas morning, wanting and waiting for the biggest and best present yet. There he was walking toward me wearing a black three-piece designer suit with the top two buttons of his still-crisp shirt undone. His tie was hanging around his neck, and he had his jacket over his shoulder.

I ran toward him, jumped into his arms, and wrapped my legs around him. Our lips attacked each other's. If I had my way with him, I would have shoved him down in the middle of the airport terminal, torn his clothes off, and fucked him crazy.

"Beautiful as ever, Miss Harper," he said with the sexy tone.

He was too good to be true, but I didn't care. I wanted to get to the bed and breakfast as fast as I could, tear his clothes off of him, and have my way with him.

We went to the car rental place, and of course he had to pick the most extravagant one that was available. People would for sure know there was an out of towner in. And most people didn't like that. Rich people where I grew up spent their money on pickup trucks, not Mercedes and BMWs. Even Aidan, Sofia's husband, had a pickup. Everett chose a brand-new Lexus GX470. Flashy as ever.

"Hurry up, let's get a room," I said with a smile from ear to ear.

"Always so pushy, Lyla?" he said playfully.

"Only with you, Everett" I replied, winking at him.

Our hands had been interlocked since the moment he arrived. It was his way of claiming me, letting everyone know I was his and he was mine. And boy was I proud that he was mine. He came to me to save me. He was my knight in shining armor, and I was the princess he was rescuing.

We arrived at the local bed and breakfast. *Shit ... my mother's best friend owns this place.* I didn't care. I just wanted a bed with Everett in it. We walked in, and Tiffani's face lit up with surprise.

"Lyla? What are you doing here?" she asked.

"I'm in town for the week. This is—"

"Everett Brown, Lyla's boyfriend," he said, interrupting me.

This was only getting worse. The moment I went into the room with Everett, Tiffani was sure to call my mother and ask her a dozen questions. Then my mother would find out that I disappeared to a bed and breakfast with a mysterious man who claimed he was my boyfriend. How the fuck was I going to explain this all? I was sick of being cautious. I just wanted Everett to myself.

As we checked in, Tiffani stared at us the whole time. I made sure to be extra touchy feely. I wanted her to know that I could get someone as magnificent as him. He was mine, and I wanted everyone to know it.

We got into our room, and before he had the chance to put his bags down, I pulled him toward me, our lips meeting.

"Has anyone ever told you how amazing you are, Miss Harper?" he asked as our kiss ended.

"I believe so, Mr. Brown ... you," I replied.

I took his lips back to mine, kissing him with my hand making its way to his ass. Gosh, it was perfectly chiseled. I could stroke it all day. I ripped his shirt off, with buttons flying across the room, and stood admiring his flawless stomach. My hands then made their way to his front, unzipping his pants. They dropped to the ground quickly. I then pulled down his designer boxer briefs.

Shit, I thought. I did well enough affording Victoria's Secret once a year. Luckily I wore a cute pair of pink boy-cut underwear. I knew he loved boy cuts and the way my ass looked in them.

He gently laid me onto the bed, leaning up for a moment, admiring me once again. He truly made me feel good about myself. He gave me a reason to live again. He lifted my arms up and pulled my black shirt over my head. He then unhooked my bra, and my breasts were bare, free, and in his hands.

Our lips met once more as he lay on top of me. I was without a shirt but still in my skinny jeans and pink wedges. I needed to get out of them soon.

"Slowly," he said in a loving tone.

We spent forever kissing with our bare chests together. I wanted him so bad it hurt. I pushed him off of me, twisting him around so he was lying on the bed. I unzipped my pants and removed them along with my wedges so I was only in my underwear.

"Take them off of me, please," I said.

"Gladly."

He removed my panties with grace. *Is there anything this man can't do perfectly*, I thought, *except to choose me? Go away, negativity*, I shouted to myself. I didn't want to ruin this perfectly amazing, erotic moment. Definitely one of the best in my life. Every moment with him was.

I lay next to him, and he flipped me to my hands and knees, spreading them further and further apart. My muscles ached from being stretched so, but it felt so good too.

A loud pounding interrupted us. We looked at each other.

"Don't stop, please. I dead bolted it. I don't give a fuck who it is. I want you inside me, now," I said.

He said nothing but did exactly as I asked. The pounding did not interfere with the erotic moment, this beautiful man taking me from behind, and it felt oh-so-good. I felt like a goddess, his goddess.

After releasing myself loudly, he followed, shouting my name. I lay on my stomach with him on top of me on my back. Our skin sweaty. It felt amazingly good. The pounding didn't stop. No one said anything. It was getting hard to ignore. He peeled himself off of me and put on his boxer briefs.

"Who's there?" he asked.

"Sgt. Davis Moore with the county police department."

Fuck, it's him, and he's here, and Everett is going to lose his shit.

Chapter 16

"EVERETT, STOP. PLEASE don't do anything stupid," I pleaded. "Stupid? Stupid is coming back to this shithole town, Lyla. Stupid is running into this asshole that I have to deal with. That's what fucking stupid is!" he yelled.

How could this be? A perfectly good moment, gone too quickly. Tears again started to stream down my face, taking my black mascara and eyeliner with them. I looked like a hot mess, but I didn't care. I just wanted him.

"Stop, Lyla, please. I'm sorry. I'm just so pissed off right now. I need to answer the door. I won't do anything foolish, I promise," he said.

He then proceeded to wipe away my tears with his thumbs and kiss me sweetly. It was his way of apologizing again. So he couldn't be perfect all the time. I was okay with that. I was far from perfect, and he had no problem accepting me for who I was.

"Yes?" Everett said while answering the door only in his boxer briefs.

I knew he did this on purpose. It was his way of making Davis jealous, even more so after hearing me during our fucking session that happened just minutes before. I made sure that I was hiding in the bathroom when he answered the door. I didn't want to come face to face with that asshole again, not tonight. It wasn't the right time.

"Is Miss Lyla Harper here? I'm a friend of the family and also a cop, and her mother asked that I go and look for her," Davis said in his cocky cop voice.

"First off, yes she's here with me and safe. Second, I hardly believe that after what her family finds out about you that you'll remain a friend. And third, you must have some fucking nerve showing up here trying to steal her once again. It isn't going to happen, bud. Finally, if you put one more fucking hand on her ever again, I'll fucking kill you. Do we have an understanding?"

"Excuse—"

"No, no excuses, fucker. You heard what I said, and I mean it. I'm not some small-town douche bag that you want to fuck with. I'm an attorney, and I live in Chicago and deal with bigger assholes than you on a daily basis. Watch yourself. That isn't a threat. It's a warning," Everett said sternly.

"Get the fuck out of my doorway!" Everett shouted as he slammed the door in Davis's face.

"See, no big deal," he said as he came back into the room.

I couldn't believe it. Within the past few weeks, I meet this gorgeous, hot, intelligent, wealthy man who was willing to accept me, scars and all, pleaded with me to give him a chance, to give us a chance, we fell in love, and he traveled over four hundred miles to be with me? *I'm one lucky girl, considering the circumstances.*

"Come, now," he said, pointing to the bed.

I did as I was told and felt sexy as hell, naked from earlier. I pranced onto the bed. He pushed me to my back, spread my legs apart, and rocked my world with his lips like it had never been rocked before.

"Holy shit," I panted.

"Nice, eh?" he said proudly.

I wondered where he learned to do that. My mind wandered for a moment, wondering how many women he had been with. How was he not married or engaged yet? Was it really destiny like he said? I was starting to believe it, believing in myself for the first time.

"What now?" I asked.

"I have no idea, Lyla. I'm just happy to be here with you."

"What about your work?"

"I've taken the rest of the week off—personal reasons. Everything is fine there. Don't worry, baby."

"I think I need to face my family."

"Tomorrow morning?" he asked.

"Yeah, I'm dreading it, but I have to."

"I'm coming with you," he stated.

"I'm not sure if that's a good idea. I haven't told them about you or us. They'll be so quick to judge me for jumping into this so fast with you. How will they understand?"

"Who cares, Lyla? Nothing else matters now. We've found each other—remember, destiny? As long as we have each other, nothing else matters. At least that's how I feel."

"Me too," I said, wrapping my arms around him.

"Tomorrow you'll meet my family," I said.

Chapter 17

MORNING CAME TOO soon. He was facing me, sleeping, so perfectly, so angelic. I could stare at him forever, but I needed to face my family. It was going to be difficult, to explain everything to them, but I had to. To move on with Everett. He stirred slightly, and his eyes opened slowly.

"Good morning, Everett."

"No, perfect morning," he said, pulling me closer.

I was convinced that I would never get enough of him. He was intoxicating. I never wanted to be without him. I couldn't imagine my life any other way. Maybe my past brought me to him. Maybe God brought him to me, to save me and help me understand myself. I tried my best to wrap my head around everything, trying not to over think things. I had never felt truly loved like I had when I was with him. He completed me, he was my other half, and I was his.

He started rubbing my scars, and the freshly scabbed cuts. It was the first time in years that I didn't cringe when they were touched. After all, they had only been touched by me. His mouth made its way to my belly. He planted sweet, soft kisses on each one. There were dozens.

"Promise me something," he urged.

"Anything," I returned.

"Don't ever hurt yourself again, Lyla," he said as tears welled up in his heavenly green eyes.

"You gave me a reason to love myself again. It's the first time in my life that I have truly accepted myself, good and bad. I uh, lo—"

"I love you, Lyla," he said softly, with tears now down his face.

"I love you too, Everett," I said, sobbing. "Make love to me, please."

He took me into his arms, kissing me everywhere. We couldn't get enough of each other. He touched me in all places, imperfections and all. I clutched his back as he made his way on top of me. My nails dug into his back as he thrust himself into me. We both were crying from the overwhelming emotion, the emotion of love that we both deserved so much. It was love, erotic, intoxicating, perfect joy. I was his, and he was mine forever, and I finally believed it. We gave each other all the love that we had. I could spend time without end in his arms, making love.

We both released at the same instant, our eyes staring at each other's.

"I love you now, always, and forever, Lyla Elizabeth Harper," he said with absolute certainty in his voice.

"I love you more than anything, Everett. Please never leave me."

"Never."

We lay next to each other, touching, kissing, smiling, and talking about nothing of depth. It was refreshing. As much as I dreaded it, I had to see my family that day. They deserved an explanation. Even though it would be hard for them to hear, I had to make them understand.

I looked at my phone. Holy shit! Seventeen missed calls, six voicemails, and ten text messages all from Mom, Rick, Rosalynn, and Garrett. I opened the first text from my mother.

Lyla Elizabeth! You're worrying me to death. Please call me. I think you have a lot of explaining to do.

The next one was from my sister:

God damnit, Lyla, what the hell is going on? Please don't do this to me again. I cannot bear it. Call or text me so I know you're safe. And who's this man that Mom said you're with? Tiff called her in a panic. Call me so I know you aren't lying in a ditch somewhere. I love you no matter what.

Shit, shit, shit! I didn't want to listen to the voicemails, to hear the worry in my family's heart. I sure as hell was going to delete all of them, especially the ones from my brother. He was overly protective and was probably in a drunken rage. He probably said things he didn't mean. I called my mother first.

"Hey, Mom, I'm fine, please don't worry. I'll explain everything in detail. I'll be at your house shortly."

"What is all this about? You were doing so well, and you come home for the first time in four years, slap the police chief's son in a crowded bar, and storm off. I then get a call from Tiffani telling me you checked into the bed and breakfast with some mystery man. I can't go through this again, Lyla."

"Mom, it's not what you think. Please don't say those things. I promise you'll have a much better understanding of me once I tell you everything. Trust me. I know it's hard for you to, but please trust me. Call Rosalynn and Garrett, tell them I'm on my way over to your house. I need to tell them about things too; they also deserve an explanation."

"Okay, just so you know, your sister is less than happy with you. She was in tears all night. Thankfully she has Aidan."

"Thanks, Mom. I love you. Please make sure Rick is home too."

"Oh, honey, you have no idea how pissed he is. He nearly had a heart attack last night. I'm sure he's looking forward to your conversation more than anyone."

"See you in a few, Mom. I love you."

I hung up the phone trying to withhold my tears. Everett looked at me, not saying a word, giving me a reassuring smile.

"Everything will be all right, honey. Remember, we have each other. With each other, anything is possible."

My heart was melting, but I finally understood and believed him. I got up, showered, and put on the clothes that I wore the night before. They smelled of smoke and stale alcohol.

"I need some different clothes. I'll change when I get to Mom's," I said.

"Take these," he said, handing me a pair of Ralph Lauren sweats and a white T-shirt.

I put them on, inhaling his smell. It made me smile. He made me smile.

"You look sexy as hell, Lyla, wearing my clothes," he said slyly.

I smiled back at him. I looked over at his naked body after he got out of the shower, proud that he was mine. He got dressed in some jeans and a white t-shirt, looking hot as ever.

"Ready?" he asked.

"As ready as I'll ever be," I replied.

I hopped into the luxurious Lexus GX470 rental car. There were so many buttons; I didn't know what half of them did. He punched my mom's address into the GPS. I told him the directions, but apparently he was so used to GPS he decided to use it. The drive only took about fifteen minutes.

He turned right into my parents' long drive.

"Nice place," he said.

I nodded, my mind distracted from the conversation I would soon have with my whole family. Holy shit—my mother and

Rick were waiting for me on the front porch, sitting in their matching high-back wooden rockers. Cramping and nausea took over my body. I wanted to throw up. I wanted that feeling of imminent doom to release itself from me. I wasn't ready to revisit the situation that transpired between me and Mr. Bad Cop, but I had no choice. There was no turning back now. It was now or never.

"Lyla, what the fuck!" screamed Rick before I even had the chance to land my feet on the gravel drive.

"Who the hell is this? God damnit, Lyla, did he hurt you?" shouted Rick.

"Rick, stop it! Please! No, he hasn't hurt me. It is not what you think. Give me a chance to explain," I said, hugging him and crying.

"Who are you?" asked Rick in a condescending tone.

"I'm Everett Brown, Lyla's boyfriend from Chicago. I've heard a lot of great things about you and your family. Nice to meet you," he said nicely with his hand extended.

Rick reluctantly shook his hand with suspicion in his eyes.

"Everett, this is my mother, Marguerite," I said.

"Nice to meet you, Marguerite," he said with a grin on his face and joy in his voice, his green eyes lighting up.

"Please call me Marge," she said, reluctantly shaking his hand while giving me an uncertain look.

"I think we should head inside. Garrett, Rosalynn, and Aidan are anxiously waiting. You have a lot of explaining to do. Garret was furious last night, almost got into a fight with some random bar fly. It was a mess. We've all been worried sick," she said sadly.

I followed my parents inside with Everett's hand tightly wrapped around mine. He gave me a gentle squeeze.

"What the fuck, Lyla! Who the hell is this guy?" exclaimed Garrett.

He got up briskly and headed toward me and Everett with rage in his overprotective eyes.

"Stop, Garrett! Now!" I shouted. "Sit, everyone. I have a lot to tell you. This is Everett, my boyfriend from Chicago. It was him who urged me to talk with everyone, so I would appreciate it if you would stop the judgmental looks this minute. Second, I know what you're all thinking, and trust me, it's far from the truth."

Everyone sat on the large brown leather sectional situated across from the fireplace. *How do I start this conversation off?* I thought. *Where do I start?*

"This is going to take awhile," I said. There they were again, the tears. I couldn't withhold my sobs. I sat there crying, trying to get the courage to revisit one of the most traumatic events of my life, the stealing of my innocence. Everett hugged me tightly with everyone's judgmental stares. I didn't care. I knew everything would be all right in his embrace. I was ready.

Chapter 18

"FIRST OFF, I know I have disappointed you all at some time or another in my adolescent and adult life. Maybe after you hear what I have to say, it may make more sense. It isn't going to be easy to hear, but it's time I stop hiding it, and telling you all is a way to turn the page and move on with my life. I can't hold onto it anymore."

Everett kept a tight squeeze on my hand, his way of showing support. I did not even know where to start, how to tell them. Before I could decipher the words in my head, I blurted it out.

"I was raped by Davis Moore the summer before senior year on my eighteenth birthday. He stole my virginity," I said, my eyes stuck on the bricks of the fireplace.

My mother fell to her knees, sobbing. "What?" she screamed.

Rick stood quickly, embracing my mother, pulling her into his arms. He had such hurt in his eyes.

My sister, brother, and Aidan remained seated, wide-eyed. No one said anything for what seemed like forever. Instead, my sister stood, taking me into her arms and giving me the tightest hug.

"Lyla, I um, I don't know what to say," Rosalynn said sadly.

It became too much for her to withhold her sobs. She started crying. Garrett's face turned crimson with rage. His fists were clenched, and his knuckles were white. Aidan looked at my sister as if he were trying to take away the pain that she felt because of me.

"I'm so sorry, everyone. I shouldn't have told you, to worry you all like this. I'm sorry I'm such a burden to you all and now to Everett."

I walked out the front door. No one came after me. I didn't expect them to. What I had just told them would take awhile to digest. I sat on my mother's wooden rocker, lighting a Parliament cigarette. I contemplated a lot of things at that moment.

I wondered if my failed suicide attempt made more sense to them, and why I did it senior year. I should've known better than to take too many Benadryl. That obviously was a botched attempt. For a minute, I wished I had taken the whole bottle of Xanax instead, knowing that would have been effective. Maybe it would've been better that way, if I had been successful.

I heard the front screen door shut and heavy footsteps. I didn't bother to turn around and see who it was. Surprisingly, I wasn't crying. I was numb. It was him. My Everett. He had sadness in his face. His green eyes seemed a paler shade. I wished I hadn't dragged him into it all. He deserved better.

"You okay?" he asked.

"I don't know anymore."

He grabbed my hand and kissed it.

"Everything will be good, Lyla."

"I'm not so certain anymore, Everett," I said straight-faced.

"I am. I'm sure about you, about us, about our fate to be together. I'm absolutely sure that I'll help you through this. I want nothing more than to make you happy, Lyla Elizabeth Harper. I'll do everything in my power and in my being to do so. I love you more than life itself," he said as he gently squeezed my hand.

I looked at him, and he was quietly crying. My heart broke for this man. He loved me so, feeling my pain and my shock.

Willing to do anything and everything for me. When was I going to understand that? When would I accept it? I needed to stop being so selfish.

"Please don't cry for me, Everett, please. I love you too. I'm so sorry that I brought you into all this. I don't know what to say or do anymore. I feel so lost. I thought telling my family would be a relief, but it has only made me feel worse, for I have put a tremendous amount of baggage on their shoulders. What do I do now?" I pleaded.

"Lyla, when will you understand that it was not your fault? First, you need to realize that. Everything will fall into place. I promise. We'll get through this together. Your family loves you so much. You didn't put baggage onto their shoulders. You simply told them the truth. Maybe they'll be more understanding of you now."

"It's too late to press charges. I've just caused a huge uproar, Everett. Rick is friends with Davis's father. What will happen now? I don't want to make a big deal about it. This is killing them. I know it. I shouldn't have said anything. You were right; coming home was a mistake. Let's go. I want to go now. Let's go home."

"Lyla, running away will fix nothing. You cannot run away. You said yourself that you needed to face this to heal and to move on. Running away will only make things worse."

"I want to leave! Now!"

I was crying uncontrollably at that point. My mother came onto to porch.

"Lyla, my dear daughter, please don't cry. It's killing me. I wish you would have told us sooner. I wish so many things. I'm so sorry that I have been so hard on you. This all makes sense now. This is not your fault," she said with generosity.

As I was sitting there, it all clicked. I needed to stop being an emotional mess first. Then I needed to admit it and move on. In order to do that, I needed to help my family. The tears started to slow, and my life became clearer with each passing second.

"Mom, I'm fine. I'll get through this. I needed you all to know so you would not be disappointed in me anymore. It was selfish of me to hide it from you guys and put you through all those years of my troubles. I'm sorry about it. I cannot change it now. All I can do is move forward. If it weren't for Everett, I would not be standing here right now. He has helped me more than you can comprehend. I do not want to dwell on this. I want to put it past us all," I said.

She said nothing. Instead she hugged me tightly and kissed my cheek. I did not want pity from anyone, just understanding. At that moment in my life, that is exactly what my mother gave me.

I worked up the courage to walk back inside and confront the big elephant in the room.

"I don't want pity from anyone. I just want you all to understand, even though that should not have been a reason for my behavior and acting out all these years. I want to put it past us all and move forward. For the first time in my life, I feel safe. Everett, I have you to thank for that. I have a reason to live again. I need everyone to remain calm and think clearly. Please don't make any rash decisions that you'll regret. Being in a small town full of politics is hard enough, and I don't want to add this debacle to it. The past is the past, and I'm over it. I need you all to promise me that," I said.

"How can you let this go, Lyla?" Garrett asked sternly. "I'll get that fucker!" "Garrett, stop! This is enough. I've told you I want to put it in the past and I want it to stay there. Please don't do anything stupid!" I exclaimed.

"How, Lyla? How am I supposed to react when I see him? I can barely contain my pure anger and rage now," he replied.

"Please, for me, Garret. I don't ask you for anything, but I'm begging you for this. For me and my future. Please."

Without a word, my brother stormed out of the house, hopped into his Dodge pickup, and sped away. Sudden terror and uneasiness pulled into my belly.

"He's going to fucking kill him!" I cried. "Mom, do something! Rick, please!"

Within a split second, Rick picked up his cell and made a call. As much as he wanted Davis to rot in hell, he did not want my brother to end up in prison. He was making a warning call to Davis's father. He was going to tell him everything.

Chapter 19

Rick went on to the porch for privacy as he called Steve Moore, Davis's father. It felt like he was out there forever. I wanted to barge out there and listen to the conversation. After all, it was about me. But I realized that I no longer needed to fight the battle alone, like Everett said to me a few days before. I wasn't unaided anymore. I had an army that was willing to fight alongside me. It was a refreshing and new feeling.

Rick moseyed back inside, his footsteps heavy.

"So?" I said.

"Davis is on duty, driving somewhere in the county. Steve tried reaching him by his cell, but there was no answer."

"What did you tell Steve?" I asked.

"I told him everything," replied Rick with certainty in his tone.

"How did he respond?"

"How any father would, knowing what their son did to an innocent girl. He's furious."

"Did you warn him about Garrett?" I asked.

"Yes, he's called in a few extra deputies to be on duty to look out for Garrett. I told him how angry he is. I'm sure he went to King's to let off some steam. Let's not jump to any conclusions," said Rick.

Even though Steve Moore was the retired sheriff of Shelton County, he still had some pull within the force.

"Well what are we waiting for? Let's go to King's," I urged.

Everyone gathered their things, and we got into separate cars, heading to the town's tabernacle, the holy place for gossip and trouble.

We arrived there in no time, as none of us were paying any attention to the speed limits. We obviously were not worried about being pulled over considering the recent events that had transpired.

I was relieved to see Garrett's Dodge pickup truck in the parking lot at King's Bar. I got out of the car before Everett even had a chance to put in park. I ran inside, and to my relief, Garrett was sitting in the corner with his head on the table and several empty beer bottles in front of him.

My heart ached for my big brother. It hurt me to see him like that. I hated that I had something to do with his latest indulgence. He had always been protective of me, but I was scared that he would use it to the extreme.

The Garrett that I knew before the corps wouldn't have acted in this manner. He would have probably cussed and threatened Davis to no end, but they would be empty threats. Now, I was actually scared that he would act on them. He was short circuited and angry. I wished I could take some of his pain away. The pain the he suffered in order for his country to be safe. His friend, Trent, wasn't as lucky.

They had been best friends since elementary school. They both joined the corps at the same time, serving in the same platoon in Iraq. But one would not return. Garrett had not been the same since. I wanted to help him heal, but I instead opened his wound again, and I had a lot of guilt for it.

"Garrett?" I said.

"What?" he snapped.

"Please talk to me. I'm so sorry. I shouldn't have told you about it. If I could take away all your pain, I would. The last thing I wanted to do was to add to it. It will be okay. I'm okay. But I need you to promise me that you're not going to do anything that you will regret. We all love you and want you to be safe," I said, trying to reassure him.

"God damnit, Lyla! I ain't gonna do anything, okay? I just want to get out of this shithole town. I envy you for being able to do that, ya know?" he said, trying to change the subject.

I could feel everyone staring at us from afar. They would not come too close, afraid to ignite the fire.

"You can do anything that you put your heart and mind to," I replied.

"Have a beer with me, sis. Everyone, come and sit. Let's put this shit behind us."

I let out a sigh of relief. I felt his pain for me, for I felt pain for him the same way with his struggles.

Everyone gathered to sit around. There was silence for a while. I decided to break it.

"So, everyone, want to share a pitcher?" I asked.

Rosalynn let out a loud cackle. "Oh, Lyla, really?"

"Why not?" I giggled.

I went to the bar and ordered a pitcher. I returned to glazing eyes, wandering eyes, and thoughts. I felt better, but I felt like I made everyone feel worse. What had I done? I placed the pitcher down on the table and filled everyone's glass to the rim.

I raised my glass. "To new beginnings."

"To new beginnings," everyone said in unison.

We sat there drinking, talking, and eventually laughing as if the whole afternoon had never happened. Maybe it was my wishful thinking or perhaps everyone was willing to put it behind them for me.

Everett grabbed some change from his pocket and headed toward the jukebox. He sat there for a few moments deep in thought. He picked some songs and came back toward the table.

"May I have this dance, Miss Harper?" he asked in a lovely voice.

"Here?" I asked.

"Yes, here and now."

It was only four o'clock, so the bar was nearly empty. I agreed and extended my hand into his. Even if the bar had been packed, I wouldn't have cared. I didn't care about anything when I was in his arms.

"I love you. I picked this song for you," he whispered to me, then giving me a gentle kiss on my neck below my ear.

The sweet tune of Coldplay's "Fix You" came out of the speakers. I, again, was lost in the words, the feelings, and his encirclement. It was as if the world was motionless, and it was just me and him, my lover, my sweet Everett. I knew he didn't want to change me. He only wanted to help me fix what had broken inside my soul.

He twirled me, kissed me, and sang to me, *"Lights will guide you home and ignite your bones, and I'll try to fix you, and high up above or down below, when you're too in love to let it go, but if you never try, you'll never know, just what you're worth ..."*

I couldn't help but cry for joy, for this man in my arms had saved my life and let me know that I was worth something. At the end of the song, he dipped me and passionately kissed me, our tongues tangoing in perfect symphony.

I heard the whole bar applaud us. I wasn't embarrassed and didn't blush, because this beautiful man in front of me, holding my hand and my heart, was mine forever.

Chapter 20

BEFORE I KNEW it, it was nearing nine o'clock. We all had clearly too much to drink. We decided to call it an evening as more people began to come into the bar. Mom was planning on having everyone over for lunch the next afternoon. Rick had spoken to Steve Moore again on the phone. Steve talked with Davis, and Davis went off the handle denying everything.

He returned his cop car to the parking lot and had not been heard from since. Steve told Rick not to worry, that he was probably going to the neighboring county where one of his ex-girlfriends lived. I tried my best not to be concerned, to put it in the back of my head, but I was scared.

"You're mine the rest of the evening, Lyla," said Everett.

"I can hardly wait," I whispered to him, smiling ear to ear.

We got into the Lexus rental car, and before I gave him the chance to start it, I pounced onto his lap, kissing him with every ounce of energy I had. This man under me had forever rehabilitated me. He gave me faith, courage, and acceptance in myself. That was something no one had ever even tried to do for me before.

His body responded to mine, kissing me back with an equal amount of energy. When I finally pulled away from him, we sat looking into each other's eyes and souls.

"Can you even give me a chance to get to the bed and breakfast?" He laughed.

"I'm finding it more and more difficult to contain myself around you, Mr. Brown."

He had his hand on my leg the whole ride back to the bed and breakfast. I was anticipating his touch in other places, making me tickle everywhere. I couldn't wait to get Everett into our room and tear his clothes to pieces, making him mine again.

The drive seemed like an eternity. Finally we arrived at our destination. He parked the car and got out to open the door for me. No man had ever been so courteous to me. Everett was such a gentleman, and I loved him for that. He took my hand and helped me out of the SUV. When my feet were planted on the ground, he lifted my chin so I was looking up at him.

His features were beyond flawless.

"I love you. I loved you the moment I saw your amazing brown eyes, perfect face, and gorgeous black hair. But I love what is in here most," he said, laying his strong hand over my heart.

He placed a sweet kiss on my forehead. I wanted him to make love to me like he never had before. I wanted to spend that evening like it was my last to live.

He picked me up and carried me over the threshold. He placed me ever so gently on the bed and then took a step back to look at me. The anticipation was overwhelming, and I could hardly bear to be anywhere except in his embrace. I yearned for the feeling of him and me as one.

He took a step closer to me, placing his hands on the hem of my shirt. He pulled my shirt off with poise. His hands then made their way to my back, unsnapping my bra with two fingers. I was sitting in front of him, bare chested and free. I was his, and it felt superb.

He moved down to the top of his Ralph Lauren sweatpants that I was wearing, placing a thumb on each side. With a sweet and quick tug, they were on the floor. I wanted to rip my underwear off myself and pull him on top of me, but the want was an amazing feeling.

"My turn," he said.

I was left in my underwear. I stood and kissed him, twirling him around so the back of his knees hit the bed. I softly pushed him down. I removed his shirt more swiftly than he did mine. I was unwrapping my favorite present. I couldn't wait to see it. I unbuttoned his jeans and tugged them off so he was fully exposed and mine.

I made my way down to my knees, our eyes never leaving each other's, and took him. He tasted so sweet I could lick him like my favorite lollipop all day. He reached up to grab my face.

"I'm not ready yet, my dear. I have a lot planned for you." He smiled.

He pulled me so I was straddling him. I still had my panties on, and the feeling was utterly erotic. His sex against mine with my underwear as a barrier. I kissed him again. It was as if our tongues were meant to be in each other's mouths. He quickly turned me so I was lying on my back. He took my panties off with his teeth, cupping my ass at the same instant. He kissed me there.

"Ah," I groaned.

Holy fucking shit. That was so sensual, another thing that I had never experienced in my life. He climbed on top of me, entering me with perfection.

"I love you. Lyla. Please love me," he groaned.

I couldn't even find words to express how I felt about him. He was giving me a beautiful new beginning. His soft thrusts were a dream. He tugged at my sweet spot. I could not take the buildup any longer and released myself around him. My body moved to its own tempo, shaking and letting go. Tears flooded my eyes. I was overcome with pure love.

"Lyla, my love," he panted as released himself into me.

He lay on top of me, still inside. I didn't want him to get up. I would be content to stay in that exact position for a lifetime. I played with his dark brown hair, twirling it around my fingers and running my hand down his back.

"Thank you," I said, breaking the silence. "For changing my life and making it whole again," I continued.

"No, thank you, Lyla, for your love and trust. It's not anything I have ever felt before."

He got up and lay beside me with our heads just an inch or so apart. We fell into a silent slumber in each other's embrace.

Morning came too soon, but it was a relief to know that last night was not a dream. I had a sweet, sleeping, angelic man sharing my bed, thoughts, dreams, and secrets. He was heaven sent. Sure, we had a run in with a few problems, but I was determined not to let anything interfere with us ever again.

He started to stir, and his heavenly green eyes opened, taking me in. I reached over and touched his stubble on his cheek. Even that was hot.

"Good morning, my love," he said.

I responded with a large grin.

"Come here," he said.

I scooted closer and laid my head on his chest with his left arm around me. I could hear his heart beating. It was a calming sensation. For a moment, it was as if our hearts were beating in unison, but then his fingers grazed my stomach, and I could feel my heart starting to race.

"I love all of you, Lyla, everything," he said while rubbing my scars and scabs.

"I love you too, Everett."

He took me softly into his embrace and held me. I swear I could have gotten off on pure touch from him. It all seemed too good to be true.

"Stop," he said sweetly.

"What?" I responded.

"I know what you're thinking, and that's not going to happen, Lyla. I know that look on your face. Stop holding me like it's the last time. Remember destiny? I'll lay my life down before I let anything between us again," he said sternly.

Lunch at my mother's house was comfortable. It was normal for the first time in years. I had my family who I adored and my soul mate that I loved more than life itself. I had never thought those moments would be possible, but they were real, and I was the happiest girl in the world.

It was Saturday, and Everett and I had one more evening together before he had to board his flight back to Chicago. I was going to head home on Monday.

No one had heard from Davis. Rick had called his father, and Steve said he had not heard from him and that he had not shown up for work. Steve did not seem worried. Apparently Davis had developed a heavy drinking problem, and Steve assumed he was in the neighboring county with his ex-girlfriend. Evidently, Davis had pulled shit like that before, going on a drinking binge and not showing up for work.

After lunch at my parents' house, Everett thanked everyone and said his good-byes. He told everyone he would see them at Thanksgiving. My heart smiled because this man wanted to be with me and my family during the holidays. My mind wandered, and I wondered for a moment what it would feel like to be Mrs. Everett Brown. *Ahh, stop! It's too soon,* I thought. *We have only been intimate for a few months!*

Everett pulled the Lexus rental car into the parking spot at the bed and breakfast. The anticipation of our intimacy was making me wet. If I could spend the rest of my life with him inside me. I could not think of anything better. I chuckled to myself.

He got out of the car, making his way over to my door, and opened it. He grabbed my hand and helped me out of the car. He placed a sweet kiss on the corner of my mouth and then winked at me. He was making me dripping wet. Surely he knew that he made me feel that way.

As soon as he unlocked the door to our room, I pushed him inside, slamming the door and bolting it. He gave me a wide-eyed smile, showing me his model teeth. I was like a cougar, ready to pounce on my prey. I threw myself at him, our mouths dancing to our own song, our tongues thrashing around each other's. I could come just kissing him, licking his full perfect lips.

"I want you now," I said, panting.

We tripped over each other's feet, and I landed on top of him on the floor. We both let out a burst of laughter.

"Well, it looks like you have me, Lyla," he said, smiling with a faint chuckle in his voice.

"I sure do," I replied. "Take your clothes off, now please."

He removed his shirt, exposing his perfection. I started kissing his lips, moving my way down his neck. He groaned. I smiled to myself, knowing that I was making him feel aroused. I trailed my lips to his right nipple, sucking gently.

"God, Lyla," he moaned.

I made my way to the other nipple and repeated my sucking. I could feel his rock-hard erection beneath his jeans. My lips slowly made their way down his abs and his happy trail. I stopped at the top of his jeans and looked up at him with my puppy-dog brown eyes.

"I believe you still have your jeans on, Everett. Should I take care of them?" I asked sweetly.

"I thought you would never ask," he replied.

He was squirming, and I was proud once again that I could affect this god of a man the way I was. I popped the top button of his jeans and unzipped the fly. No underwear again. *Fuck, I love this man.* I pulled his jeans down to his thighs, admiring his huge cock that would soon be in my mouth. It was perfect. I kissed the tip first and felt his body tremble. A low groan followed.

I squeezed it with my right hand and took all of him in my mouth, feeling his dick run down the back of my throat. I didn't gag. I wanted it more. Making him feel like this made me want to come. I sucked faster and faster, stopping intermittently and kissing the head. It was driving him mad, and I was soon to put him out of his misery. I deep throated him once again, pushing him over the edge. A salty fluid filled my mouth, and I welcomed it. I jacked him until he was done and his body relaxed.

"Wow, that is all I can say right now," said Everett.

I grinned at him proudly.

"Like that huh?" I said.

"You have no idea," he said.

I lay down next to him and kissed him.

"I love how you taste. Do you like it?" I asked.

"I love how you taste more," he replied.

He placed his hand on my hips. For a moment, I forgot that I was fully clothed. He turned me so I was lying on my back. We lay there kissing, his hands making their way down my shirt. He took his hands and gently removed my shirt. He started playing with my breasts, taking his hands and moving the lacy cups down so they leapt free. His fingers were playing with my right nipple, and he sucked on my left. I was panting, wanting a release so badly. I knew if he didn't finger me soon that I was going to spontaneously combust.

"Please," I whimpered, begging him.

He looked up at me with his piercing green eyes and dark lashes. His hand slid down my belly. He took my pants off, leaving my panties on. It was torture! His right hand made its way down to my sex. I was dripping wet, ready to release myself in any way possible, even if I had to do it myself.

"Please, make me come," I begged.

He gently slipped one finger into my throbbing vagina, touching my sweet spot. Within seconds, my body was convulsing, shaking, and my sex dripping wet. He continued to finger me, and my orgasm seemed to last forever. I was mumbling words that made no sense. Before I knew it, his fingers were out of me, and I yearned for more.

"Taste yourself," he said, placing his fingers in my mouth. I began sucking my salty arousal from his long fingers. It was hot as hell.

He took my purple boy-cut panties off and turned me over so I was straddling him.

"I want to kiss you," he pleaded.

I bent down to kiss him, and he stopped me.

"Not on these lips, on these," he said, finger-fucking me again.

"Sit on my face, now," he said.

I obliged and straddled my thighs over his face so my cunt was millimeters away from his lips. He began kissing me sweetly, and I could see my juices dripping down the side of my thigh. He licked it off. I wanted more. His tongue was moving in and out of my cunt, licking my clit, and I couldn't take the sensation anymore. I didn't want to. I let go, letting myself come again onto his lips. He sucked it out of my sex, and I felt myself coming again because the sensation was overpowering my body. He had just made love to me with his mouth.

Tears started to flood my eyes because I was sure I had felt nothing as intense as that in my twenty-three years of existence. It was pure and perfect. He looked at me with my vagina resting on his chest.

"You taste much better," he said, smirking. "I love you forever," he said wiping the tears from my cheeks with his thumbs.

I felt his erection with my hand. I scooted back and took him with my left hand. I put him inside me.

"Love me, please," I begged.

I rocked back and forth on his cock, coming again. The tears never left my face. They were tears of joy, eroticism, and love … all overwhelming but in a good way. I was sure after the past weeks with Everett that we were meant for each other. He soon released himself into me, pouring his love into the most intimate part of my body.

"I love you," I said, falling over him, and before I knew it, I fell into a sweet slumber in the arms of the man I had fallen in love with.

Chapter 21

I AWOKE IN the middle of the night. I looked over at the digital alarm clock on the nightstand next to the bed. It was three o'clock in the morning. Everett was still sleeping sweetly beside me. I lay there staring at him, swearing to myself that he was heaven sent. I was sure that if he hadn't come into my life when he did that I would've taken my own life soon after my second problem.

I began to think of all the bad things that I encountered throughout my young life. For the first time in my life, I wasn't sad about any of it. I was relieved that I finally felt good about myself. I had to love and accept myself before I allowed anyone else to love me. And I wanted Everett to love me so badly that I realized what I had to overcome. It wasn't my past events; those were just bumps in the road. I had to overcome my insecurities. I had to love myself, and I did.

Everett started stirring in his sleep. He gave a half smile, and I realized he was dreaming. I smiled to myself and hoped he was dreaming of me and of us. His bright green eyes opened, and they were once again piercing me to my core.

"What are you doing up, angel?"

"Woke up, couldn't fall back asleep. I was watching you sleep. You smiled," I said shyly.

"That's because I was dreaming of you," he said proudly, pulling me closer.

He laid my head on the safest place I knew, over his heart. I was happiest with him and was sad that he had to leave that afternoon. I knew we would only be a part one day, but it saddened me. I could spend every waking moment with him. My eyes grew heavy, and I fell into another peaceful slumber.

"Fuck," he said, panting, spilling himself into me.

Tears again welled up in my eyes. This time they were tears of sadness. I was going to have to say good-bye to him in a few hours. I knew he had to be back home and at work Monday morning. I was thankful that he had taken half of the week off to be with me and deal with my issues.

"Don't cry, baby," he said, kissing me on the cheek.

"I know I'm being silly and emotional, but I'm going to miss you. We've slept together every night for over a week. I'm going to be lonely," I said.

"We will be together tomorrow," he said, reassuring me.

Fuck. I was being clingy. I didn't want to push him away. He probably needed some space from me. He had endured quite a lot the past week with me. I was sure he needed some time to digest it all.

"What's wrong, Lyla?"

"Nothing. I was just thinking that I'm probably being too clingy. I'm scared that I'm going to push you away with all my bullshit. I don't know why I'm being so sensitive and crying all the time. I became a pro at hiding it for so many years. I'm sorry. I don't know what's gotten into me," I said, wiping my nose on my sleeve.

"Don't apologize, honey. I dread being away from you just as much as you don't want to be away from me. You aren't being clingy. This is what happens when you fall in love. You want to be with that person all the time," he responded.

"Have you ever been in love before?" I asked him.

"No," he said.

I wanted to believe him, but it seemed too good to be true. He had so many good attributes; it was hard for me to fathom that tons of women hadn't fallen in love with him.

He knew better than to ask me if I had ever been in love before. He knew that my view on men and love had been tainted.

"How do you know then—I mean if you've never been in love before?"

"I don't. It's just my view. I don't want to leave you. I love you. I want you to believe that, Lyla. It will kill me if you doubt that. I would do anything for your love," he said as he started to softly cry.

My heart was in his hands, and at that moment, I knew I had his heart in mine.

Four o'clock came too soon. I followed him to the regional airport in my car. I was going to spend the last night in town with my mother and sister. We had planned on having a girls' night drinking wine and watching cheesy eighties chick flicks like *Pretty in Pink*. As much as I didn't want to leave Everett, I was looking forward to spending some time with my mother and sister.

Everett returned the car to the car rental place and hopped into my old Toyota Corolla. I was a bit embarrassed considering his car, but I knew it didn't matter to him. I parked in the tiny parking lot adjacent to the terminal and got out. We made our way into the airport hand in hand. I didn't want to let go. I was being ridiculous. Within twenty-four hours, we would be together again. I was planning on leaving early in the morning to be home at a decent hour.

"This is not good-bye, Lyla. It is see you tomorrow," he said, grabbing my chin.

I couldn't say anything. I instead kissed him, invaded his mouth passionately. My hands were around his waist, and his were in my hair. We kissed for what seemed like a split second. The loud voice disrupted us over the intercom. It was his boarding call.

"I love you, Lyla. I'll call you when I arrive home safely."

"I love you too," I said.

As he walked away, I blew him a kiss. He shot me a million-dollar smile, and my heart melted for the trillionth time the past week. He had made me whole again. He had let me love not only him but myself.

I made my way back to my car and turned it on. I was listening to "Almost Lover" by A Fine Frenzy. It was no longer my song for him. He was my absolute lover, and I was determined to have him as mine forever.

A few cigarettes and songs later, I pulled into my parents' driveway. I saw my sister's brand-new Toyota Sequoia in the driveway and was excited to get our girls' night under way. I missed them so much and felt a pang of guilt for not spending as much time with them as I should.

I walked into the house, and my mother and Rosalynn were sitting on the sectional listening to music and drinking chardonnay.

"Lyla dear!" my mother exclaimed.

I laughed to myself. Rosalynn had already gotten her tipsy. She was adorable when she drank but had a tendency to get a little emotional. A trait that my sister and I both inherited. I was hoping that our conversation would remain light throughout the evening, but chances were slim to none.

"Hey, Mom," I responded with a big bear hug.

"Ros!" I said as she came over to me, kissing my cheek.

"Wine?" my mother asked.

"Of course!" I replied with a cackle.

We sat for the next hour or so on the porch. We had finished a bottle of wine already, and I had smoked a lot of cigarettes. Rosalynn snuck a few, which was funny. She used to smoke all the time when she worked as a nurse but quit when she met Aidan. You'd be surprised how many nurses smoke.

Our conversation had remained light for the most part. They, of course, had a million questions about Everett. I told them how we met and how he sang to me as we danced. I was sure of one thing—that I was never going to tell them about Michael. That was something that Everett and I had to deal with on our own.

"Well, have you fucked?" Rosalynn asked.

I gasped, slightly embarrassed.

"Oh come on, Lyla, don't be so modest. You know that I didn't wait till your father and I were married."

No, I didn't know that. I thought my mother was this perfect little Catholic girl who did everything the right way, opposite of her youngest daughter. Relief struck me, and I learned otherwise.

"Well … uh," I stammered.

"You have! Spill it, sister. I want all the details!" yelled Rosalynn.

"Keep your voice down. I don't want Rick to hear any of this!" I exclaimed. "What do you want to know? Gosh, this is embarrassing. I don't want to be having this conversation with you two right now. You know that we have, so there's nothing more you need to know," I replied. I could feel my cheeks rushing with blood and knew I was blushing horribly. "Besides, we make love. We don't fuck, Ros."

"Oh my! My little sister is finally falling in love!"

"Not falling—*fell* in love," I said.

My mother tried to stifle her tears but couldn't any longer.

"Mom, don't cry. Why are you crying?" I asked.

"It's just, well, everything you've been through. You deserve to be happy. I'm glad you finally are, Lyla. I love you, sweetheart."

"Thanks, Mom. Happiness is an understatement. He knows everything about me and loves me for me. He's helped me to believe in myself again and love myself. It's the first time I've come to terms with things and allowed myself to love," I said.

We spent the rest of the evening dancing to music and drinking wine in the living room. Rick was smart enough to spend the evening in the man room watching Sunday Night Football and drinking beer with Garrett.

Before I knew it, it was ten o'clock. I was ready for bed but realized that I had left my toiletry bag at the bed and breakfast. I was a bit tipsy but able to drive.

"Hey, Mom, can you call Tiff and tell her I'm on my way over? I left one of my bags there."

"Sure, sweetheart. Are you sure you can drive okay?"

"Yes, Mom, I'm totally fine. Trust me. I should be back within the next half hour or so."

I grabbed my keys, wallet, and pack of cigarettes and headed to my car. I started it and turned on Black Keys radio on Pandora. I was listening to "Chop and Change," loving their music. Ten minutes later, I pulled into the bed and breakfast and went into the main office.

"Hey, Tiff!" I said cheerfully.

"Hey, Lyla, here you go, sweetie. The cleaning lady got it from your room. Tell your mother I said hello and we need to have lunch soon!"

"Sure thing, Tiff. Thanks again!"

I opened the door and headed over to my car. I had parked under a large pine tree. The pine needles and other leaves covered the pavement, an omen that fall was coming. I loved fall. It was my favorite time of year. Football, sweatshirts, and bonfires. Those were the good memories I had at home. I wanted to have more of them. I was determined to come around more. I loved my family so much and wanted to be part of their life here too. I made a pledge to myself that I would visit as often as possible.

I went to get the keys from my purse to unlock the door and saw a shadow to my right. Before I could turn around, I had a horrendous pang of pain in my head and saw only darkness.

Chapter 22

I WAS DREAMING a wonderful dream. I was thirteen, and Rick had taken all of us on a camping trip to the Smoky Mountains. I saw a million things at once ... mom laughing her beautiful laugh, Garrett tossing the football with Rick, Rosalynn singing to herself with her portable CD player, me dancing along to my sister's voice. It was a happy memory.

I awoke with a sudden jolt. I did not recognize anything around me. I had a terrible pain in my head and around my face. My nose was running blood, and it was difficult to breathe. My mouth was duct taped shut, and my nose was clearly injured. I was in the woods somewhere but did not see any familiar surroundings.

I tried to move my arms, but they were immobile behind my back, secured by twine rope that was tied too tight. I could feel the roughness cutting and burning into my skin. My body was rested up against a tree. I was mortified when I looked down and saw that my jeans were off my body and my legs were separated by force. One ankle was tied to one small tree and the other one tied to another tree opposite. My ankles were bleeding. The rope had torn into my flesh.

I was in pain everywhere, from my head down to my ankles. I felt abused and vulnerable, mostly confused. What had happened? Who had done this to me? Why me when things were finally going well for me for the first time in my life? I thought God had given me a break when he brought Everett into my life—and now this? Was he testing me again? I didn't think I was strong enough to endure much more. I decided that it was time to give up. I closed my eyes and passed out hard from the pain.

I AWOKE TO a hard slap to my face. Sudden terror overtook my body when I saw a familiar face. It was Davis Moore, my first problem and probably my last. I knew he was going to kill me. I was ready to give up. Fighting for so long had become exhausting. I was ready for God to take me. I was ready to be within his comfort.

"Wake up, you fucking bitch!" he screamed, hitting me violently on my head again. He then ripped the duct tape off my mouth, taking part of the skin of my lips with it.

"If you scream, no one will hear you. It's completely useless to try," he said.

I said nothing to him. I did not want to give him the satisfaction of a fight. I knew he got off on that shit, and just because I was giving up did not mean I was going to give in.

My eyes met his hazel eyes, burning with rage, fury, and pure madness.

"Have anything to say, Lyla? Sorry for starters?" he asked.

I remained silent. I wasn't going to give that bastard the satisfaction of my tears or pleas. I had accepted that it was my time to leave my body and be with God. At least I had made peace with my family and given Everett all the love I had.

"You want to play the hard way, eh? Fine with me. I came prepared. You fucked with the wrong person. If you were to keep your fucking, pretty, little mouth shut, none of this would have happened. I'm not only doing this for myself, but it seems you've pissed a lot of people off Lyla ... not just me. This just means that I'm twenty thousand dollars richer, and I get the satisfaction of watching you be punished by me ... tortured by me ... for ruining my life and my career. Hope you're ready, my darling," he said, laughing and then tilting my head back, licking my neck.

I was mentally blocking out his torture. I was numb, and my mind and body were already in another place. It was somewhere more peaceful among God and his angels.

He ripped my T-shirt off so I remained in my panties and bra. I knew what he was about to do since I had endured it before. The difference between the first time and my last was that this time I was going to die. I wasn't sure if I was frozen because of the overwhelming amount of blows he had given me to the head or if God was helping me. Kind of cliché considering the conditions, but I knew God was with me during my torture.

I was ready for it to be over, but I knew Davis was going to take his sweet time with me. I knew he would rot in hell. There was no way that he was going to get away with something like murdering and raping me. I know my family and Everett would fight to find me. They would fight for my justice.

"What should I do with you first, Lyla? I have so many good memories of us. I bet your skanky-ass cunt isn't as tight as it was when you were eighteen. If you were smart, you would've stayed here in town. We could have ended up together, ya know. I could have given you what you wanted. But you had to act like you were something and move to Chicago.

"I can't believe you had enough nerve to bring your fucking Ivy League asshole boy toy here. Did you think I wasn't going to find out? Did you think for one second that I would be okay with it?

"Ya know, the other night at the bar, I really thought that we may have been able to start over. But then you had to go and be a little bitch again and slap me. You opened up a very bad can of worms, my darling.

"Then I got a call from Michael the next day. I was so fucking pissed off at you that I agreed to take care of you when he offered me twenty thousand bucks. He was the one who called me a few months ago and paid me a hefty chunk of change to dig up all your misfortunes. I told him that there wasn't much but told him about your minor consumption.

"Then I find out you're fucking his stepson. That just put more fuel to the fire. I wanted to fucking kill him, but I promised Michael that nothing would happen to Everett."

I was absolutely beside myself. It all made sense to me now. How Michael knew everything about me and about my past. He had called the county police department and by chance talked to Davis. They had apparently had some sort of exchange and realized that I would be better off dead to them. They did not want to risk being exposed. It all made sense now. I was relieved that nothing was going to happen to Everett, and I knew Davis was not dumb enough to hurt my family.

I remained silent, which just pissed him off more. He pulled my bra down so it was around my stomach and grabbed my breasts, violently pulling my nipples. I cringed but refused to cry or scream.

"This is not good enough for you? Harder?"

He pulled on my nipples even harder, and the pain was overwhelming. I felt a warm liquid running down onto my stomach; both of my nipples were bleeding from his abuse. His hands ran down my stomach, and his fingers made their way into my panties. I was dry, and he forced three fingers inside my sex. My body jerked back from the pain, but I remained tear-free. My face was blank and emotionless. I felt tearing in my sex, and as he pulled his fingers out of me, they were covered with blood.

He slammed them into my mouth so I tasted my own blood. I wanted to bite down onto his fingers but relented because that would be something he could get off on.

He untied my ankles and flipped me onto my stomach. My mouth was pressed into the dirt. He began a series of violent blows to my back, moving down to my ass. Punching, slapping, hitting in every way possible. I didn't dare make a sound. I heard the ominous sound of his zipper and the tearing of a condom packet.

He slammed his dick into my sex, thrusting a few times and then pulling out. He then thrust it into my ass, and the pain was all too familiar. I was overcome with pain and sadness and felt my world closing in … it was sudden blackness as I passed out.

I AWOKE, SPRAWLED out on my belly with my hands still tied behind my back. I could feel blood pouring out of my ass. It felt as if I were bleeding from every orifice.

"Decide to wake up, sleeping beauty?" he said, grinning at me and turning me over so I was lying on my back with my hands still tied behind myself.

He had a buck knife in his right hand and a machete in his left.

"Which do you prefer, my dear Lyla?"

I remained silent as I had the entire ordeal. I didn't care. I was ready for him to put me out of my misery.

He took the buck knife and held it to my throat. He grazed it down my neck and stopped at my breasts, making several cuts on my breasts, nipples, and areolas. The knife began to move down my belly, and he laughed as he skimmed over my scars. He pulled the knife back and pierced my stomach. I vomited from the pain and was sure that I would pass out. But no, I remained conscious. He drew the knife back for a second time and stabbed again and again.

He then took the knife down to my sex and cut me there. The pain had become too much ... sudden darkness turned into light. All the pain had left my body, and I was suddenly at pure peace. I could see myself laying there on the ground, bleeding and dying. Davis wiped his knife off on his cargo camouflage pants and put it back in the holster on his hip. He kicked me several times. He did that to make to be sure I was dead. He then spit on me and left.

Chapter 23

I T FELT AS if I were in a dream or some sort of limbo. I could see myself lying there in the dirt, struggling to breathe and stay alive. I wondered why it was taking so long for me to die. I felt no pain, no agony, and no struggle. I was just sitting there watching myself bleed.

Things started to get hazy. I was in and out of seeing myself below. Then, again, blackness. I was sure that was my end. I heard the melancholy tune "If I Die Young" by The Band Perry in my head.

I AWOKE GASPING for air. I was confused. I thought that I had died, but I was still alive in the moment, seeing my bleeding breasts and body. I tried to fill my lungs completely with air but struggled with each breath. I started to think of my sweet Everett, our first time making love. I thought about my family and all the good memories I had of them.

I started to get angry. Something deep in my gut was telling me to fight. To rouse all the cells in my body and battle to live. I wasn't sure how I was going to do it, bleeding to death with my hands still tied behind my back, but in that split second, I had decided that I wasn't going to let Davis Moore or Michael Thomas win this fight. It was my life, and I deserved happiness. I wanted the happily ever after with Everett. I wanted the perfect house with a well-manicured lawn and a white picket fence. I wanted three kids. I wanted a life, and I had to fight for it.

I had severe tunnel vision, but I struggled to my feet. My legs felt like Jell-O, and I wasn't sure how I was able to stand. I'm sure it was the adrenaline rushing through my veins. I stood, stumbling in the darkness of the woods with my hands stuck behind my back. I was naked, bleeding, dying, and determined.

I had a rush of energy run through my body. I began running as fast as my feet could take me. Dodging tree limbs while stepping on sharp sticks and jagged rocks. Oh no, the darkness again … and it was black and nothing.

"Hey! Hey! Can you hear me? Wake up, Lyla! Open your eyes, damnit!" yelled a familiar male voice.

I heard movement and commotion, but I couldn't open my eyes. They were too heavy. I was breathing small shallow breaths, pain with every inhale and exhale, but I wasn't ready to give up. I wanted my Everett.

"Stop! Please! Stop! Stop!" I yelled.

"Lyla, it's all right. I'm helping you. I've called the police, and the ambulance is on its way. Hang on, sweetie," said Kenny, the bartender and owner of King's.

He was dressed in full-out hunting garb. Camo shirt and coveralls topped off with a bright orange hunting hat. He must have been hunting deer and come across my naked and mutilated body. Thank God. I just had to hang on a bit longer, but it was becoming more and more difficult.

Kenny carried me to the desolate road where I heard shrieking sirens. It was now daylight, and I wondered how long I had been lying in the woods. It didn't matter since I had help now.

"Lyla, dear, who did this to you?" asked Kenny.

I fought to let words roll off my tongue but summoned the energy and whispered, "D-Davis."

"Oh my God. Hurry the fuck up, Clark! She's bleeding out" screamed Kenny to one of the paramedics.

I felt the hard back of the stretcher and the warmth of a blanket and drifted into a peaceful stagnation.

I opened my eyes to two paramedics frantically working on my breaking and dying body. They were applying a horrid amount of pressure to my stomach, and the pain was so great that I vomited everywhere, struggling not to choke on it.

"Suction, Clark!" yelled the other paramedic.

They stuck the suction catheter into my mouth, expelling all the vomit from my mouth to make sure that I didn't aspirate.

"Hold on, Lyla. We're almost there," said Clark.

"Mom? Mommy? Where are you? Mom!" I cried.

"The detectives have contacted your family. They're on their way to the hospital, Lyla. Hang on a little longer. We're almost there," said Clark.

I couldn't do it anymore, and the familiar blackness took over my body. I was so tired.

Chapter 24

I FELT A squeeze on my left hand. I tried to open my eyes, but they were too heavy. I tried to talk but felt a foreign object in my throat. I was entangled with a lot of wires, and the constant beeping noise was giving me an overwhelming headache. I must have moved in some sort of way because I heard a stirring in the room.

"Lyla, honey, it's mom … can you hear me? Squeeze my hand, my darling daughter, if you can hear me. I love you so much, honey. Stay strong. Feel the Holy Spirit with you. Squeeze my hand, baby, please," said my mother. I could hear her soft sobs.

I squeezed her hand.

"Rosalynn, Aidan! She squeezed my hand!" yelled my mother.

"Lyla! Thank God. Hold on a little longer. I love you. Please hang on," cried my sister.

"Lyla, it's Aidan … you're in the ICU. It's Tuesday, and you had surgery to repair your injuries. You have an endotracheal tube in your throat that's helping you breathe. Your vital signs are stable," he said in a professional tone.

I'm still alive? Thank the Lord. I couldn't believe that I had been unconscious for three days. I wanted my Everett to be with me. I needed him more than my next breath. I wanted to hear his voice, for he had strengthened me, and I knew if I had him that I would pull through and heal physically.

I tried to pull my hands up, but they were restrained. My body started thrashing, and I was bucking the ventilator. I knew that it was protocol to restrain patients who were on the ventilator so they didn't pull the tube out. I had heard enough stories from my sister to know that. But the feeling of being restrained was bringing back the horrendous memories of my last encounter with Davis. Terror rushed over my body.

"Lyla, stop. You're safe. It's all right. Calm down," said Aidan.

"Honey, there are cops guarding the ICU. You're safe. They're going to find Davis. Relax, sweetheart. We will not let anything happen to you," said my mother in a serious tone.

I felt at peace and fell asleep or passed out. It was hard to know the difference at that point.

TIME MEANT NOTHING to me. It could have been hours, days, or weeks. I opened my eyes. The fluorescent lights were blinding, and my throat was beyond sore. There was no tube in my mouth anymore, and my hands were free. I was still hooked up to a million monitors, and the beeping noises continued, still giving me a headache. I realized I was alone and let out the loudest scream that I could.

"Lyla? You're awake! Thank God!" shrieked my mother as she came running in my room. "It's fine, darling. You've never been alone. I was just out at the nurses' station speaking with Aidan."

"What day is it? Where's Everett?" I whispered.

"It's Friday, sweetie. I called Everett as soon as I realized you were missing. He's been here the whole time by your side. He just left a few moments ago to use the restroom."

"Oh, Mommy," I cried.

"Hush, my sweet daughter, you're going to be okay. You have always been a fighter. You're going to be fine."

I looked down at my stomach and saw that it was bandaged with a tube coming out of my right side. It was attached to a bulb-like device that was full of a pale red color. I was in a tremendous amount of discomfort but did not care. I was just happy to be alive. I was grateful that I decided not to give up.

A few moments later, my sweet Everett walked in. His beautiful green eyes were full of tears that he could no longer contain. He let out a loud sob, running to my side and touching my hand like I was a breakable porcelain doll.

"Don't cry. I'm alive," I croaked.

Fuck, my throat hurt.

"God, thank God. I love you so much. I died a million deaths since I got the news. Thank God," he sobbed, kissing my hand with his perfect lips.

"Have they found him yet?" I asked, referring to Davis.

"No, sweetie," replied my mother with worry in her tone.

"They'll find him. I promise you that. If not, I'll find him," said Everett.

I nodded my head.

"Honey, when you're feeling up to it, the police need to speak with you. I know it's going to be difficult, but you need to tell them everything you can remember about what happened, okay?" said my mom.

"I'm ready to tell them now," I said. "But I want Everett to be with me. Is that okay?"

"I'm not ever going to leaving you again," said Everett.

He gave my hand a gentle squeeze. I smiled at him.

"Lyla, there's something you need to know," said Everett with his head down.

Oh shit, this was bad. He could not even look me in my eyes. What could be as bad as what I had endured? My mind wandered, and I got a horrible feeling in the pit of my being.

"What? What is it?" I urged.

"Everett, no. Not yet ... she can't handle it," my mother pleaded.

"She needs to know," he replied.

"Will you two stop talking as if I'm not here? What the hell are you guys talking about?"

"Lyla, um ... we, uh, you were pregnant. But ..." Everett trailed off, crying into his hands.

"But what?" I said, trying to withhold my tears. "What do you mean were?" I asked.

"Your body endured so much trauma and blood loss, and you lost the baby. You were only six weeks along. I'm so sorry, angel. The doctors are hopeful that you're able to have more children but could not give us a 100 percent guarantee because of all the uh ..." He trailed off again.

I was speechless. I cried, sobbing uncontrollably. Davis had taken my baby away from me. I was furious. Pissed off. I wanted to jump out of my bed and go and find him myself. I wanted to tie him to a tree like he had to me and beat the living shit out of him. He took away an innocent baby, my and Everett's baby. It was not fair.

I didn't speak. I began to wonder what my baby would have looked like. He would have had my skin and black hair with Everett's perfect green eyes and full, pink lips. But I would never know.

"Why?" I said to myself out loud.

"I know, baby. I'm so sorry," cried Everett.

"The ob/gyn spent several hours in surgery repairing your wounds. You had extensive vaginal wall tearing and damage to your cervix. Your perineum was stitched, and the physician said if you're able to have more children in the future, you're going to have to have a caesarean section and a cervical cerclage to make sure you don't go into pre-term labor. I'm so sorry, honey. I wish I could take it all away," explained Everett.

"I want to talk to the police now!" I said, trying to digest all the information I was just given.

Chapter 25

THIRTY MINUTES LATER, Detective Miller from the county police department came into my hospital room. He was a short, bald man with a protruding stomach and a serious look on his face. I was not intimidated but felt at ease in his presence. I was ready to tell him everything. They obviously knew I was raped considering the amount of trauma I had to my private areas. And Davis took my baby away from me and my lover. I wanted them to find him, and as much as it pained me to think of the ordeal, I was ready.

"Good afternoon, Miss Harper. I have a few questions that I need to ask you. Are you feeling up to it?" asked Detective Miller.

"Yes."

"If you do not mind, I would like some privacy," he said, looking at Everett.

"I would like him to stay please," I said to the detective.

"I suppose if you feel that it will make you more comfortable."

Over the course of the next hour, I described my night of terror. I was very explicit in the details of my rape and his torture to my entire body, including my sex. I told the cop about my very first encounter with Davis Moore when I was eighteen. As much as I didn't want to tell him about Michael Thomas, I had to. After all, he was the reason that I was laying in the hospital bed. He was the creep that paid Davis to kill me, even though I was sure that Davis would have done it for free.

I described my life in Chicago and my internship. It was a complicated mess, the triangle of Everett and his stepfather. I told Detective Miller in great detail of my anal rape by Michael Thomas. I gave him every detail he asked for. Then the hard part came. I had to tell him in front of Everett that Michael paid Davis to kill me and rid me from the world forever.

"Davis told me that he was contacted by Mr. Thomas and was offered twenty thousand dollars to have me taken care of. Apparently Michael had called the county police department when I was interning there to dig up dirt on me. Their paths crossed by chance, I suppose. They realized that I had become a problem for the both of them. Michael has an indispensable amount of money, and he wanted me dead for fear of exposure. Davis had already been exposed and had nothing left to lose," I said, looking over at Everett. His face was stone cold, filled with pure anger.

"That's it," I said, expressionless.

"Lyla, I really appreciate your statement. If you can think of anything else, please do not hesitate to call. Here's my card with my office and cell numbers on it. I'll answer day or night. We'll get them. Stay strong," said Detective Miller.

I gave him a gentle smile. I looked over to Everett at my right, and his expression was the same. Stone-cold anger. It pained me that I had brought him into all this. What was going to happen to Michael? I was positive at that point that his mother would be devastated and would hate me.

"Say something, anything please," I said.

"I've got to go make some calls, baby. Don't worry," he assured me, kissing me on my scratched forehead.

"What about your mother? She's going to hate me," I sobbed.

"Lyla, don't worry about any of that, please. We're just going to have to figure a lot out along the way. Like I said to you weeks ago, nothing else matters since we have each other." Everett came back into my hospital room, not revealing much about his recent telephone calls. I was feeling uneasy. I felt as if he was hiding something from me.

"When can I leave the hospital?" I asked.

"You have a CT scan scheduled for tomorrow morning to make sure there's no more active bleeding in your abdomen. That's what the drain is for. It's called a JP drain. The doctors said once that's under control, then they can remove the drain and monitor you for a few more days."

Man, was he on top of my health. He must have been at my side the entire time. He really was in love with me. I was so confused. I was unsure of what I was to do with my life after this debacle. Do I stay home? Do I go back to Chicago? I needed some guidance. I didn't know what to do with myself. I was struggling to convince myself that I wasn't a burden.

"I'm ready to go home, though I'm not quite sure where that is. What am I supposed to do now? Where do I go?" I asked, tears flooding my eyes once again.

I was tired of crying all the time. It seemed as if I had done more crying in the past two months than I had my whole life. Maybe it wasn't a bad thing. I knew my coping mechanisms were unhealthy for so many years. I had, after all, internalized a lot.

"Where do you think you'll be most comfortable, baby?" asked Everett.

"I don't know … that's the problem. I don't know anything—where to go, what to do. What about my apartment in Chicago?

All my stuff is there. Your job and life is there. Oh God, Everett, what about your job?"

"Hush, baby, my life is here with you ... where you feel safe. Wherever you are is where my home is. I'm never leaving you again. Ever."

"So do we stay here or go back to Chicago? I don't think I can leave my mom right now. Not after everything that's happened. It wouldn't be fair of me to expect you to stay here with me. I understand if you need to go back to Chicago. You've worked so hard for your career. I cannot ask you to give that up for me."

"I don't care about the life I had there. It was nothing, meaningless, unfulfilling, and empty until you. You're my life, my love, my next breath. You make me a better man. I love you more than anything in the entire universe, Lyla. It will not be difficult for me to find a job here."

"Are you sure?" I asked while quiet tears streaming down my battered face.

"I have never been surer of anything in my entire life until I met you."

"What about all of our things? Our leases to our apartments? Your car? There's so much to be figured out," I said, starting to worry and get anxious.

"Baby, I'll take care of it all. Please don't worry. You need to focus on getting stronger. The process is not going to be easy, and I'll make sure I'm there with you. I promise to be there for you, for all the good and bad. Happy and sad times. I'm in this for the long haul ... forever," he said as his eyes welled up.

"Love doesn't even describe the feelings I have for you. I'm so sorry about our baby," he cried as his hand reached and gently rested on my belly. "God damn, this is not fair," he sobbed.

"I'm so sorry, baby ... I'm so sorry" he said, with his hand still over my empty and tattered womb.

"Please don't cry, Everett. I don't understand any of this, but I'm sure that as unfair as it seems, it's in God's plan for us. We will see our baby again one day," I said, trying to stay strong for him.

After all, he had remained as tough as a gladiator through the whole thing. Despite my condition, I wanted to remain strong for him. He was affected just as much as I was.

"Look at me please. We'll get through this. We'll be happy. I refuse to let all this interfere with our future. I want to be happy with you, forever and always. It's not going to be this hard all the time. It will get easier every day. We have each other to lean on for support," I said.

"God, you're one strong woman. I love you so much. After everything, you're the one trying to make me feel better. I'm a shitty lover. I should be holding your hand while you're crying," he said, wiping his tears away.

"It was your baby too, Everett. All of this affects you as well," I responded. "I'm so ready to get out of this fucking hospital!" I said, trying to change the subject.

"Soon enough, baby. Soon enough," he said, stroking my vacant belly.

Chapter 26

THE NEXT FEW days were physically exhausting and painful. I was sore from head to toe but didn't care much since I would be on my way home in the next few hours. Everett had taken care of our leases and set up the moving company to pack and move our belongings to Kansas. His car would follow as well. In the meantime, we are going to stay with my parents until we found a house.

He was spot on about finding a job. He landed a gig with a small firm dealing with mostly family law. The pay was not nearly as much as what it was in Chicago, but he didn't seem to mind. The cost of living was significantly lower than in Chicago. He was going to start in two weeks. He was waiting on getting his law license in the state of Kansas. I was secretly happy that I would have him all to myself for a few weeks before we started our life together.

The detective from the county police department still hadn't found Davis. His father, Steve, swore that he had absolutely no contact with him since he tried getting a hold of him after Rick broke the news to him about what had happened to me. The police officers pulled his cell and home phone records, and it turned out that Steve was telling the truth. Who knew where

Davis was; he had enough money to run across the country and start a completely new life.

I wasn't quite sure why, but I had pity on the man that destroyed my life and murdered my baby. I was sure he would end up in hell. Maybe that's why I felt sorry for his soul. Maybe he would turn his life around and one day be sorry for his doings. He not only wrecked my life, but also Everett's, my family's, and his poor family. His father was genuinely a good fellow, and I couldn't imagine enduring the heartache his father was.

I was deep in thought when a middle-aged woman with a soft face entered my room. She was dressed in bright pink nursing scrubs.

"Lyla, I'm Kelly, your nurse. I have to go over some discharge information and look you over before you can go home."

"Sure," I said eagerly. I felt like I had spent eons in the hospital. I wanted the comfort of my parents' home. I was ready to snuggle with my sweet Everett on the sectional next to the fireplace while he whispered sweet things into my ear, making me smile. I wanted my happiness again, and I was determined to get it back and put this mess behind me.

"Here is a list of the prescribed medications that the doctor wants you on. I have called them all into the Rite Aid on Third Street. The pain medication, as you know, may make you a bit sleepy, but that's okay. You're going to need plenty of rest," she said.

"The antibiotic needs to be finished. It is important to do so, so the infection doesn't return. Take that one with food.

"Here's a list of your restrictions," she said, handing me a piece of paper that seemed a mile long.

"No lifting anything over five pounds for at least six weeks or until the physician clears you. No reaching above your head. No exercise. And no sexual intercourse for six weeks or until your physician examines you at your follow-up appointment. It may be longer than six weeks or a bit shorter. Everyone heals differently."

Six weeks without sex? Was she crazy? How was that going to be possible with Mr. I'm the Hottest Man on the Planet, also known as my boyfriend, sleeping next to me every evening? That was going to be hard. It was going to suck! I began to wonder if I would ever enjoy sex again after all the damage that had been done to my private areas. Anything was possible, I supposed, especially if you were as lucky as I had been to find true love. It wasn't just physical, but also very emotional for us every time we made love.

"Finally, here are the instructions for your wound care. The JP drain has been removed, and the dressing needs to be changed twice daily or when visibly soiled. It may leak a straw-colored fluid for a few days. That's normal. If it starts draining blood, yellow, or green, you need to call the doctor immediately, as that's an indication of infection and active bleeding. Your other surgical wounds are secured with staples. The physician will remove those at the end of the week. Those can be open to air, and you can shower normally. Here's your appointment card with the date, time, and location of the doctor's office. That appointment is when he will remove your staples. Here are the other cards with your appointment times for your follow-up with the ob/gyn," she said, handing me several cards.

After signing a million pieces of paper and a quick assessment of my body by the nurse, I was ready to go home! Finally!

"Hey, beautiful," Everett said as he gracefully walked into my hospital room.

I smiled sweetly at him, appreciating everything he had done for me. He began gathering all my flowers and belongings and sat them on a cart.

"Ready, baby? Let's go," he said.

He helped me into the wheelchair and pushed me down the hall to the elevators as the nurse followed us with the cart full of my flowers and belongings. We made our way down to the lobby, and I was stunned to see his Mercedes S600 under the hospital canopy. He really was on top of his game! He already got his car home, found a job, and arranged for our things to be delivered by the end of the week. *God, I love this man.* I was the luckiest girl in the world.

He loaded everything into the backseat of his luxury sedan and helped me into the front seat. I was exhausted from the small amount of ambulation. I knew right then and there that a long recovery was an understatement. Would I ever be back to my old self? I prayed that I would.

The drive to Mom and Rick's house was quiet. Everett's hand remained interlocked with mine as he occasionally stroked my scratched knuckles. We were both obviously deep in thought. Who wouldn't be after all the shit that had happened? I swear my life was worse than a soap opera. I was ready for it to settle down.

I wanted the police to catch the fuckers who did this to me, but I didn't want that to consume me. I knew that they were both too smart to try again. Davis was probably halfway across the country, and I was sure Michael lawyered up and wasn't talking. He was smart, and I knew he would try to find a way out of it.

Twenty or so minutes later, we turned into my driveway. The smell of the pine trees lining the road made me smile. The fall air was brisk and cool, and I was happy regardless of the recent circumstances. I was just glad to be alive in the arms of my lover and soul mate and with my family who I knew loved me to pieces.

I was sure that God had me endure hell to appreciate myself. It was my new beginning, my fresh new start. I was determined to be content and happy ... no more self-destructive behavior, no more self-medicating the pain through alcohol, no more cutting. Done. Forever. I had a reason to be a better person, and his name was Everett Patrick Brown. He was mine.

Chapter 27

MY MOTHER WAS patiently waiting for me on her rocker on the front porch. Rick was situated next to her in his rocker, smoking a cigar. Rosalynn's Sequoia was parked, as well as Garrett's pickup truck. My stomach started to ache. I was worried about how my brother was dealing with things. He had been so angry since he got back from the war. The last thing I wanted was this recent fiasco contributing to his new binge. I hoped with all my being that we would all be able to work through it in a healthy manner, but the chances of that were slim to none.

Everett put the car into park and ran over to my side of the car, opening my door. He reached in and gently helped me into a standing position. I was slightly dizzy but gathered myself and planted my feet on the gravel drive.

"You okay, baby? Want me to carry you in?" he asked.

"For heaven's sake, Everett, no. I can do this. It just may take a few minutes," I said with a chuckle.

He was just too sweet and caring to me. He placed his arm around my waist, steadying me as I attempted to walk. A few minutes later, I climbed two stairs to settle on top of my parents' great wraparound porch. My mother flooded toward me, hugging me softly.

"Gosh, Lyla dear, I'm so happy you're home and safe. God has truly answered our prayers," she said, kissing me on the cheek.

"Thank you, son, I don't know what we would have done without you. It's apparent how much you care for my baby girl. Thank you again," said Rick.

He started to tear up but restrained them from falling to his cheeks. I had never seen him cry or get emotional like that. He was a true man's man, never showing much emotion. He held his hand out to shake Everett's, and when Everett took his hand, he gave him a big bear hug. I smiled from ear to ear. It meant a lot to me that my family loved and appreciated him just as much as I did.

"Come in, honey. We have everything ready for you. Let's get you inside and situated. I cooked some homemade marinara sauce with spaghetti and garlic bread. I know how much you loved your Nonnie's marinara sauce recipe. How does that sound?" she asked.

"Wonderful," I responded.

I was famished. It was the first time I felt really hungry. Hospital food wasn't exactly gourmet. And with all the pain I had been in, the last thing I wanted to do was eat. I had clearly lost a significant amount of weight. My hips were less curvy, my legs and ass smaller, and my breasts less full.

Everett held my hand and helped me over the threshold into the house. The smell of the marinara was mouthwatering. My eyes started to tear, and I broke out into sobs.

"Oh, honey, what's wrong? Are you okay?" asked my mother as she practically ran to my side.

"Oh … it's nothing, Mom. The smell of the marinara sauce reminds me of Nonnie. I just miss her and Nonno, that's all. I miss them so bad," I said, still crying.

"Shh now, sweetheart. They are always with you. They would be so proud of how strong you are. Now come and eat. You have some visitors," she said.

Everett led me into the formal dining room. I never realized how truly exquisite the room was. It was a pale mint green color with ivory white wainscoting. A large pine table was in the middle and sat twelve people comfortably. An antler chandelier hung from the ceiling, and several paintings of lakes and waterfalls hung neatly on the walls.

I sat with my whole family, enjoying a great homemade Sicilian meal. I ate more than I had in weeks and laughed more too. My sister's boys were there, and they could make anyone go from a sour mood to pure happiness in an instant. I was sure that evening that my happiness was returning, and I was not going to allow it to fade away. I was going to continue to fight for it for the rest of my life. I would not tolerate anything to come before it. Ever. Again.

After lounging on the sectional next to the fireplace in the arms of my lover, I began to grow sleepy. My body was beyond tired, and the pain was returning. I needed another pain pill.

"Want me to tuck you in, angel?" Everett asked.

"Sure. I need my pain pill first."

He returned with my medicine and a glass of water. I took it in one gulp and was ready for bed. I went to stand up, and he stopped me.

"Please, baby, let me," he said as he smoothly picked me up.

He carried me into the spare bedroom downstairs that my parents had set up for us. It would be easier for me than to climb stairs to my old bedroom. I was relieved. I didn't want to revisit the place that had so many bad memories attached to it.

Everett swiftly pulled back the duvet and placed me on the bed. He pulled the comforter up to my chin and kissed me on my forehead.

"Sleep, my sweet angel," he said.

"Come to bed with me, please," I urged.

"I will shortly, baby. I have to make a few phone calls and answer a few e-mails."

I didn't want to question what the calls or e-mails were about. He had done so much for me the past couple of weeks. I didn't want to be a nagging menace and intrude. But deep down inside, it was bothering me. What could he possibly be hiding from me? Was it Michael? Had he spoken with his mother since the attack? Had the investigators talked with her or Michael? My mind was racing a million miles a minute, and my head started to ache. The pain pill soon kicked in, and I fell into a safe and quiet slumber.

I awoke and looked at the digital clock on the nightstand. It was past midnight, and Everett was not in bed with me. I grew anxious and summoned the energy to swing my legs to the side of the bed. I stammered to my feet and made my way to the living room. There he was. Sitting deep in thought with a glass of hard liquor in his hand. He must have sensed my presence because he jolted to the standing position, hurrying to my side.

"What are you doing up, Lyla? Do you need something?" he asked.

"I woke up, and you weren't there. I want you in bed with me. I sleep better when you're next to me. Are you okay? Is everything all right?"

"Yes, baby. Don't worry. I have all of our ducks in a row. Have a few houses I want to show you online tomorrow. You can choose which one you want," he said, rubbing my face.

"Okay," I responded.

I was still worried. I knew there was something he wasn't telling me. Now was not the time or place to bring it up.

"Come to bed with me please," I urged.

"Sure, honey," he said, grabbing my hand and leading me into the bedroom.

He tucked me in once again and lay next to me so our faces were nose to nose.

"I love you, Everett. I can never thank you enough. You saved my life."

"No. Thank you, Lyla. You've given me a purpose in life. You're my purpose in life."

"Kiss me please," I urged.

"Lyla, baby, that probably is not a good idea."

"Well kissing was not on my list of restrictions. Please. I need you, Everett. Please."

His green eyes pierced mine. I knew his lips wanted mine. I wanted—no, I needed to taste him again. I had to. I moved closer to him so our mouths were almost touching.

"Kiss me please. I need to taste you again. It has been too long. Please," I said. "I need you, Everett. Let me taste you again. Let me let you taste me again."

Finally, with our eyes locked, his full lips met mine, kissing me sweetly. I offered him my tongue, stroking his and sucking on his bottom lip. He started to pull away, but I would not let him. I continued the flawless motion of our kiss, our tongues sweeping against each other's as we occasionally sucked each other's lips.

He pulled away from me.

"Damn it, Lyla, I just can't do this," he said sadly.

"Why? Do you not see me the same anymore, Everett?"

"Of course I do. It's just, well, it's impossible for me to contain myself around you. I want you so badly that it hurts."

"Then have me. Do what we can. Let me try something, please."

My lips were aching for his. I wanted them against mine again. I needed to feel them again.

Chapter 28

WE SAT THERE nose to nose. He was contemplating the situation. I was not. I just wanted him. I needed him.

"Taste me again, please," I said.

He couldn't take it anymore and took my face with both of his hands.

"You're beautiful, strong, intelligent, and mine. I want you to be mine forever. I love you, Lyla Elizabeth. You're an angel sent to me. I want you now and forever. Always remember that."

Our lips met again, resuming the rhythm of kissing, sucking, and stroking tongues. I started to tingle in places that I was scared were damaged forever. Thank God they weren't. I felt his full erection pressed against my thigh. I knew right then and there that I wanted to make him come even if I couldn't do it through sex.

"I want to make you come like this," I said, kissing him again, gently touching his erection through his pajama bottoms.

A deep groan roared in his throat. We continued our tango, making love to each other with our mouths as I occasionally caressed his cock through his pajamas. His body grew rigid, and his breathing became more rapid. I continued to barely touch his sex, and he pulled his head back trying to withhold his moans.

I kissed his neck, sucking beneath his Adam's apple.

"Let go, baby," I whispered.

With those words, my lover was pushed over the edge and released an orgasm solely from our kiss and me barely caressing his cock. I kissed him deeply again, grabbing his cock, welcoming the warm liquid through his pajama bottoms.

"Fuck," he said, panting. "That has never happened to me before. What you do to me, Lyla, I never want to let it go."

"Then don't. You have me forever."

"I love you, Lyla."

"I love you too, Everett. Always."

"Marry me, Lyla."

"What?" I was shocked.

I knew that we would be together forever, but I certainly was not expecting that question for some time. We had a lot of shit to get straight. And he wasn't telling me everything. I needed to know what was affecting him. I yearned for his thoughts and feelings. I wanted him to be able to talk to me about anything. After all, I had shared my entire life with him. He, on the other hand, hadn't. I didn't want to push him, but I needed to know the full extent of the *situation* back in Chicago. The *situation* that happened to be married to his mother.

"Don't you want me forever, Lyla?" he asked.

"Of course I do, Everett."

"Then say yes, say yes to being my wife." He stood up and pulled a tiny velvet box out of the nightstand.

"We need to figure a lot of shit out first, Everett. You won't talk to me about your mother. The police have not briefed me about Michael. I know this is all affecting you, and I need to know that you'll share your thoughts and feelings with me. I'm not saying now, but soon. Please give me that. I've shared everything with you. Do the same for me. I know it isn't easy, trust me."

"Okay, I will. But not tonight, angel. You need your rest. But say it. Please tell me that you will be my wife. I want to know that you're mine forever," he said, opening the velvet box.

I was at a complete loss for words. A three-carat princess-cut canary diamond ring stood before me. It was beautiful. It had tiny white diamonds surrounding the large one. It was set in platinum.

I knew I wanted to say yes, but I also needed to know what he was hiding from me. I came so close to losing him before. I didn't want to come close again. I didn't want to over think it. I responded, "Yes, yes I'll be yours forever."

"Oh my God, really? Really?"

His shaky hands placed the amazing ring on my left ring finger.

"You make me the happiest man on earth, you know that, baby? I'm going to give you the life you always dreamt of. You're always what I dreamt of, and now my dreams have come true. I love you so much, Lyla," he said with tears of joy.

"I love you too, Everett."

Chapter 29

THE NEXT FEW days went by fast. Everett and I picked out a home. I found one online and was in no shape to go see it in person, so he went and checked it out. It was a go. It was a brick ranch-style home with three bedrooms, two bathrooms, formal dining room, family room, and den with a log fireplace.

There was a large three-car attached garage and a 40x60 pole barn. A little lake was situated to the left of the house with a gazebo that would look perfect decorated with tiny paper lanterns on a cool fall night. We could drink tea, enjoying the lake. The large two-tiered back deck was ideal for hosting barbeques. I could imagine Everett over the grill, laughing with my family. It was everything I wanted.

The home came with five acres of land. We had it all, privacy, space, and most of all each other to share it with. Everett had a hefty down payment, and luckily it was vacant and move-in ready, so we only had to wait one more week to close on the house. His credit was impeccable, so that made the process much easier.

WITH EACH PASSING day, I felt better and stronger. I had my staples removed and was looking forward to my appointment with the obstetrician/gynecologist on Friday at the end of the week. Most of all, I wanted to know what my future held as far as having children. It was something I always yearned for. I never knew how much I wanted to be a mother until I met Everett. I wanted to be the mother to his children. I wasn't sure if it was going to happen with me. I was still having difficulty accepting the loss of my baby. I wondered daily what life would be like if my attack never happened.

Everett was my rock. I hoped that I was his in return. He still had failed to open up to me about his family, his mother, and Michael. The police had only my statement, which was going to be rebutted by his attorney. They were questioning my statement because of all the shock I endured and said that my mental state was questionable. There was no money trail. No withdrawals of twenty thousand dollars from any account Michael had. I knew that would happen. He was too smart and had planned it carefully.

The investigation was at a complete standstill. Everything else in life seemed to be moving forward. I was ready to move into my new home. The home I would be sharing with my future husband. We were moving in over the weekend so Rick, Garrett, and Aidan could give Everett a hand with all the heavy lifting.

"LYLA HARPER?" ASKED the plump medical assistant at Dr. Raymond's office, my ob/gyn.

I stood immediately. My nerves were running wild through all the cells of my being. I was ready to face the truth regarding my status of being a future mother. I wanted nothing more than to carry Everett's baby once again … not anytime of course, but in the future. We were to marry the coming spring, and I didn't want to wait much longer afterwards if I was able.

I entered the bright white medical exam room. There was a tiny window on the opposite wall, revealing the rainy, gray day, which I was hoping was not an ominous sign of the news I was soon receive.

"Remove all of your clothing and put this gown on with the opening in the front. Dr. Raymond will be in soon, Lyla," said the medical assistant with remorse in her voice.

I was aware that she was familiar with my story. Not only was it located in my medical chart under the H&P but also scattered throughout local newspapers. I removed all my clothing and placed the soft pink gown on my scarred body. I stepped up onto the medical exam table, patiently waiting. I began tapping my fingers, trying to stray my mind onto a positive topic. I was picturing my new home in my head, deciding where furniture and pictures would look best when a quiet knock interrupted me.

"Come in," I said hesitantly.

"Lyla dear, how are you feeling?" asked Dr. Raymond with her gentle hand out to me.

"Okay," I replied, shaking her dainty hand.

"First I'll do the physical exam to check how your healing is progressing and then we will go over everything else. Does that sound all right?"

I was positive that she had never dealt with anything of this nature before. In a shitty southeastern Kansas town, she never had had to deal with sex abuse and attempted murder victims. I was sure that my injuries were the worst she had seen.

I nodded my head and leaned back onto the hard surface of the table, feeling the exam paper crinkle underneath my thin gown. I lowered my heels into the stirrups so they would support my legs and froze. My knees were locked, and I refused to let them fall open. Tears started to fill my eyes, and I did not hesitate to let them fall.

"Lyla, I know this is very hard for you, but you're safe. I need to make sure that you're healing properly. Do you wish for my medical assistant to accompany us?" asked Dr. Raymond.

I said nothing. I shook my head no. I relaxed my hips and let my knees fall apart. I regretted not letting Everett come with me, but he had just started the previous week at the new law firm, and I did not want him missing work. I had been a big enough burden on everyone lately. It was time for me to regain some of the independence that I had lost. I could not let this recent debacle control my life. I was determined to get through it and put it in the past, hoping it would stay there.

I felt the cool air hit my sex.

"You're going to feel me touch, Lyla. It may be a bit uncomfortable," said the doctor.

I again nodded my head yes without saying a word. I wasn't sure if there were any words that I could articulate that could come close to describing the feelings I was feeling. Vulnerable, sad, unsure, insecure, and most of all unwomanly. I needed to hear that I would be able to bear children again one day. I had to hear those words.

An intense amount of pressure was placed in my vagina, and I felt a piercing pain. I nearly flew off the table as my silent sobs continued. Then as quickly as it started, it was over. She remained quiet and continued her physical exam of my abdomen. She began feeling around deeply at my internal organs. She then moved up to my scarred and tattered breasts. The scabs on my nipples and areolas were now fresh scars and a constant reminder of my brutal attack.

She scooted back, removed her latex gloves, tossed them into the trash receptacle, and took a seat on her rolling chair, jotting down notes onto my chart as if she was deep in thought.

"You have healed nicely. Your cervix is badly scarred, but I'm hopeful that will not interfere with your future pregnancies. We will need to be proactive in the future and do a cervical cerclage, as I told you before, once you have become pregnant. I don't feel any abnormalities other than that. Your perineum is completely healed, and all the stitches both external and internal are dissolved completely. I would like to schedule a follow up with an ultrasound next month just to check things out." She jotted some more notes.

"As far as your restrictions are concerned, there is no need for them anymore. You may resume sexual activity. It may be sore for the first few times that you do it, but that should go away with time. It's crucial that you use protection or we'll start you on some kind of birth control. You should not get pregnant again for another six months."

"Okay," I said. I was beyond relieved. I could deal with that news. "I guess I'll start some kind of birth control."

"I'll write you a prescription for birth control. It's a low-estrogen birth control pill. You need to take it the same time every day and use a backup method of contraception the first month after."

"All right," I replied taking the prescription from her.

"Take care, Lyla," she said and then hugged me. I was grateful for her because I knew that she helped save me and my ability to have children. I was more than eager to share the news with Everett.

Chapter 30

I HEADED BACK to my parents' house and decided it would be best if I told Everett the good news in person. It would be our last night staying with my parents, as we would be moving to our new home in the morning. We had everything packed and ready and were going to meet the moving vans at our new house at eight o'clock sharp. I was beyond excited, counting down the minutes until my lover was with me again.

Five o'clock came soon enough, as I busied myself with simple, menial tasks. I heard the tires hit my parents' gravel drive, and butterflies overtook my belly. I looked out the huge bay window in the living room and saw Everett's flashy Mercedes S600. I calmly walked onto the porch, waiting patiently for our eyes to meet.

I could hardly take the wait any longer; it felt as if every second was hours. I walked over to him, and as soon as our eyes met, my knees felt weak, and I wanted nothing more than to be held, kissed, and touched by him … my lover, soul mate, fiancé, best friend, and other half. He flashed me one of his million-dollar smiles, and I returned the smile.

"Well? I was waiting for a call. How did everything go, baby?" he asked, sauntering over to me, draping his hands around my hips so our mouths were inches apart.

"Great. She seems to think that I'll be able to have more children in the future. She put me on a birth control pill but said we should use condoms for the first month."

"That's fabulous news, baby," he said, hugging me.

"I'm so relieved," I said.

"I love you! Do you even understand how much, Lyla Elizabeth soon-to-be Brown?" He smirked.

I liked the sound of that. Lyla. Elizabeth. Brown. His in every way.

"She cleared me for sex," I said blatantly.

"Did she now?" he said.

I was trying to judge his reaction. I hoped that I could still have the effect on him that I had before. I hoped he didn't look at me differently. I wanted nothing more in the world at that moment than to feel his thick cock inside of me. I wanted us to physically and emotionally be one again. There was no waiting in my book. My parents were gone until at least ten since it was the monthly catfish supper at the VFW.

"Well, how do you feel about that? My parents won't be home till long after ten."

"I want you always."

"Then take me now," I pleaded.

I felt my nipples perk and tighten underneath my fitted T-shirt. I purposely hadn't worn a bra under my shirt or underwear underneath his Ralph Lauren sweatpants. I was hopeful that I could have him inside me.

I grabbed his hand and led him into the house. I walked down the hallway and opened the door to our room. The butterflies remained in my belly, as if it were our first time. Our eyes met and were stuck in a heated gaze. We remained silent.

I walked over to him and began unbuttoning his shirt. Once I freed all the buttons, I removed his silver cufflinks and neatly placed them on the nightstand. I took his shirt off, admiring what was mine forever. His perfectly toned chest and abdominal muscles made my mouth water.

My shaky hands made their way down to his belt. I unhooked it and took it off, wasting no time before unbuttoning his pants and unzipping his fly. I pulled them down, gaining access to his fitted boxer briefs that showed his hard length underneath. He kicked his shoes off and finished pulling his pants off. I bent down and removed his socks one by one. It was a very intimate moment for us.

I raised myself up, and he took my mouth onto his, gently kissing me, stroking my tongue and sucking on my bottom lip. I was dripping wet, as it had seemed like an eternity since I had felt this with him. He was the only person that I had ever felt this way with.

We continued our perfect rhythm of kissing as his expert hands made their way to the bottom of my shirt, skimming my erect and sensitive nipples in the process. He gracefully took my shirt off, stepping back and taking a deep breath. It dawned on me that he was admiring me just as I had always admired him. I. Was. His. Forever.

I frantically removed my sweats, tossing them across the room, and climbed onto the bed naked, wet, wanton, and his.

"You're absolutely stunning. I'm the luckiest man on earth to have you for the rest of my life. I love you," he said.

He made his way over to the bed and took his boxer briefs off, tossing them aside. I was lying on my back and let my knees gently fall apart, exposing my drenched sex.

"Fuck, Lyla. I could come just looking at you."

"Come here, please. I need you. In. Me. Now."

He climbed on top of me as if I were some sort of porcelain doll. We were nose to nose, eye to eye, and his strong hand started to skim the top of my cheek, down my sensitive neck, to my breast, and he stopped for a moment and leisurely stroked my erect nipples, sending a shockwave down my over-sensitive body. I let out a groan, throwing my head back and arching my back. His hand caressed my permanently scarred stomach and ended up at the inner apex of the thigh.

"Please," I begged.

He then slipped one finger into my sex. There was no pain, just pure pleasure, and a second later I was pushed over the edge as he fingered me and took my hard nipple into his mouth, sucking sweetly. I felt the warm liquid shoot from my sex and hit the bed.

Fuck, that had never happened to me before, but I could not control it. Before I knew it, his mouth was on my sex, sucking the shooting cum out of my pulsating vagina. I was screaming his name in ecstasy as his tongue darted in and out of my tight opening, still offering him my salty liquid arousal. I couldn't get enough and gyrated my hips up to his mouth, wanting all he had to offer.

"Oh God," I cried as my orgasm continued to ripple through my convulsing body, giving him more and more of my salty arousal from my dripping vagina.

"In me now!" I cried.

He leaned up with the shimmer of my cum on his lips. It was sexy as hell. He grabbed a condom and gently sheathed it over his hard cock. He bent down and kissed me. I tasted myself on his lips, which was a turn-on, deepening our kiss.

"Are you ready, baby?" he asked.

"Yes," I said.

He gently placed the head of his cock into my throbbing vagina and eased his hard length into my sex. It didn't hurt, but the fullness was overwhelming. He froze, but I nodded my head yes to have him continue. I wanted all of him.

He gently pushed himself into me until he was eventually balls deep. I arched my back and tilted my head back, preparing myself for another earth-shattering orgasm. I was sure I could come just looking at him. His tempo grew steady as he took my nipple into his perfect mouth, sucking and tugging. I kneaded my hands in his amazingly dark and thick hair.

"Ahh, Everett!" I screamed, coming again. I felt it come out again, pouring over his hard length, wetting the bed. His tempo grew faster and faster, making me come harder. The intensity of it was overwhelming, and tears welled in my eyes as I continued my cries for more. He took my mouth into his, stifling my screams as my nails dug deeply into his back, and with one last thrust, my lover experienced his release, breathing my name sweetly on my lips.

We lay on the bed lazily, in each other's embrace. No words could come close to what I had just experienced. I was far from embarrassed. I was actually proud to have had such an erotic and intimate moment with my soon-to-be husband. There was going to be no holds barred in the bedroom department with us. That was for sure.

Chapter 31

"GOOD MORNING, SLEEPYHEAD," Everett said with a grin on his perfectly pouted lips.

"It's moving day!" I exclaimed.

I was more than ready to start our life in our own house within the privacy of our own walls. I wasn't sure what to do next. Everett was adamant that I stay at home until I was fully healed. Even though the doctor had released me for *all* activities, he thought it would be best if I focused on our home and setting our roots down.

An hour or so later, everyone met at my parents' house to drink coffee and make plans for the day. Garrett, Aidan, and Rick were all going to help Everett move all the heavy furniture. The moving trucks were going to meet us at our new home. I was so excited.

After all the logistics were laid out by Everett, everyone hopped into their cars and made their way to our new home.

Within fifteen minutes, we arrived at 5100 Honeysuckle Way. I was sure I was dreaming. I finally had the love of my life, my family, and my future all within an arm's reach. It was everything I had always wanted. Maybe the circumstances beforehand were less than ideal, but I was sure that God had put me through everything to mold me into a stronger person.

All of our brand-new furniture was moved into our home within several hours. There were boxes in every room that still needed to be unpacked, but Rosalynn, Mom, and I had plans to place everything from the boxes to their designated place in the upcoming week.

I was more than exhausted and was relieved that everyone made the decision to skip dinner plans. Everyone else was also wiped out. I was ready to get settled in with my lover (soon-to-be husband!). I was still overwhelmed that such a beautiful man wanted to have me for the rest of our lives. There were some serious conversations to be had, especially regarding Michael.

He was still in Chicago, with his mother in their mansion, and out of jail. I couldn't believe that he wasn't locked up yet. But in the end, it was my word against his. No money trail, no surveillance footage, no phone records. Michael was much smarter than all of that. I was sure that he had this planned from the moment I stepped into his office.

I wanted to talk with Everett seriously about his mother and what their relationship was like. I had to know. It only seemed fair since he knew everything about me that I should know everything about him too. I wanted to be his support system. It seemed like I was the only one he had now. It saddened me.

Everett plopped down on our chocolate brown leather sofa with a sigh. I knew he was tired, but I was determined to address the inevitable. I had to know what was happening between him and his mother.

"Thank you," I said shyly.

"For what?" he replied.

"For doing all the hard work and moving all the heavy furniture. I know you're probably exhausted, but at least we have another day to spend together before you have to go back to work.

We can lounge around and relax … enjoy one another's company in our new house," I said, stroking his calloused hands.

"Anything for you," he said, shooting me his infamous million-dollar smile.

My knees went weak, and all I could think about was his mouth on me. I wanted him so badly that it hurt. I was addicted to him, but I was determined to get this conversation over with here and now. No more hold ups.

"Everett, we need to talk."

"What's wrong? Are you all right? Feeling okay? Was today too much for you?"

"Stop, Everett. I'm fine, seriously. But you have been avoiding this conversation for weeks now. It's only fair that I know what's going on, especially since it affects you. You keep telling me that I'm not alone. Well, the same goes for you. I want to be there for you. I want to be the shoulder you cry on and the ears that listen. I want to be the person that gives you advice when you need it. I want you to need me in the ways I need you."

"Lyla, there's not much to discuss. I've already told you I cut all ties to Chicago. There's not much more to say."

I knew he was hiding something from me. It was far from reasonable. Honesty is the best policy, at least that's what I thought was important for a relationship to grow through good times and bad. He wasn't giving that to me.

"I cannot have you hiding things from me. It's not right. I feel like this relationship is not heading in the right direction, and until you can come completely clean with me, then I don't want to talk."

At least I was standing up for myself. It hurt me to see that pained look on his face. I didn't want him to think I was letting him go. I wanted to prove a point. We had to overcome it before we said, "I do."

I retreated into the master bedroom, half expecting him to follow me, but he didn't. I curled onto the giant king-sized bed that I was supposed to share with my lover. Tears started to pool in my eyes, but I kept them behind. I drifted into an unpleasant slumber ... horrible nightmares following.

"Lyla! Lyla! Wake up, baby. It's me, Everett. You're okay! You're safe with me, baby. Please. I'm here!" he cried.

My heavy eyelids opened. My face was wet with tears that must have seeped through my eyes during the nightmare. It was another flashback, a vivid recreation of the torment from Michael and Davis. They were meshed into one horrible nightmare. I felt betrayed. He hadn't slept with me, and it was the first flashback I had since the attack. It was the first time I had fallen asleep alone.

It was the most secluded I had felt since I left Rigdon, Kansas, four years before.

Shadows of Scars and Sorrow

THE SECOND BOOK of this series will be told from Everett's perspective. Throughout the book, he will try to prove to Lyla his love, devotion, and trustworthiness by making sure he substantiates Michael's guilt. More information will unfold about Davis Moore.

Everett will eventually be honest about his relationship with his mother. Nothing will get in the way for his love for Lyla.

MARY E. PALMERIN has been writing short stories and poems since she was eight. She is married, has two boys, and currently resides in southern Indiana where she is hard at work on the next book in the Sorrow series.